Evernight Publishing

www.evernightpublishing.com

ISBN: 978-1-77233-002-1

Cover Artist: Sour Cherry Designs

Editor: Tricia Kristufek

COLORS OF US

DEDICATION

Some say writing is a solitary activity. I argue that statement. A writer's work is based on cords of emotions and threads of experiences artfully woven together to produce a story. The root of those emotions and experiences begins with the people in our lives. Whether a drive-by acquaintance, a lifelong friend, or somewhere in between, it's those people who add rich layers to our stories and make writers, well, write.

Here are just a few people who helped me along the way...

Michelle (whose portrait inspired this book): Thank you for sharing your work with me.

My wickedly talented "writerly" friends: Evie, Colleen, Deserie & Stephanie: You each contributed to this story in some way. I hope you see yourselves in these words. Your support means everything.

The Bookalicious Babes: You make me smile every day. Thanks for sharing your love of reading.

Cheyenne: Your energy, sweetness and enthusiasm inspired the Cheyenne you're about to meet.

The instructors at CKO Kickboxing, Franklin: I've never sweated so much in my life! Thanks for helping me kick my own butt and get into my characters' heads.

The galleries of SoHo: For opening your doors and answering my questions.

My editor, Trish: For your direction and keeping Hunter's hands from wandering off on their own.

Renee Bunino: For teaching me to make time to find the beauty in life.

AB and family: For being so patient while I finish this book!

COLORS OF US

McAvery Brothers, 1

Sandra Bunino

Copyright © 2014

Chapter One

Michelle woke with a gasp and sat straight up in her bed. Fear slithered down her spine as she pulled the dampened sheet to her chest. *It was just a dream. Just a dream.* Rubbing her temples, she recalled the last time she'd had a nightmare. A month ago? Maybe two. What used to be an almost nightly occurrence dwindled to one every few months. The ever-increasing time between bad dreams meant she'd come a long way from the day she'd stepped off the bus at Penn Station and started a new life in The Big Apple.

She rubbed the knot of tension under her shoulder. "Shake it off, Willis. Everyone has nightmares once in a while," she muttered before taking a deep breath and blowing it out slowly through her lips.

Sunlight streamed into her tiny studio, and the familiar morning noises of her neighbors wrapped around her like a warm blanket. The single mom with the stomping toddler in the apartment above her, the elderly man from down the hall who shuffled past her door on his way to the corner bakery, even the newlyweds next door who enjoyed a lusty morning quickie before heading to work—all provided a degree of comfort that everything was right in the world.

Stretching her arms, she caught her reflection in the mirror on the wall. Light shadows replaced the dark circles that had once resided under her eyes, thanks to sleep and her daily workout routine in her building's basement. She'd hoped to exchange sessions on the worn-out treadmill with early morning runs through the streets of neighboring Tribeca, but she wasn't ready for it yet. Baby steps.

Michelle slipped out of bed, padded across the room to her kitchenette, and ripped open a store-brand oatmeal packet. Turning the faucet knob to hot, she dumped the contents into a chipped mug and held it under the steamy water for a moment. Flakes of dried oats floated to the top as she sprinkled a packet of sugar over the meager meal. Stirring the contents together, she moved to her closet and kicked the door open. There wasn't much to choose from in her tiny storage space. A few pairs of black pants, blouses, and sweaters from the consignment store made up her work wardrobe, yoga pants and sweatshirts were weekend clothes, and one little black dress reserved for gallery events.

The metal hangers rattled as she pulled her best pair of dress slacks and black sweater from the closet and slipped them on. A quick trip to the bathroom to brush her teeth, tie her long hair into a neat bun, and swipe on some blush and lip gloss completed her morning routine. She grabbed her backpack and rushed down two flights of stairs to her second-hand bike, which was locked to the rack in the narrow lobby. Turning the numbers to the correct combination, she freed the chain from the lock and wound it around her seat. A gust of wind ruffled a few strands of hair loose from her bun as she pushed the front door open and walked her bike down the short flight of cement stairs to the sidewalk.

Mounting her bike, she sucked the cool city air through her nose and released it slowly from her mouth. The tight muscles in her back relaxed while she pedaled, slow at first, until the light changed and the cars emptied out of the side street. She pumped her feet and rode as fast as they would take her to the end of the block, enjoying the cool air hitting her face, making her feel alive. Turning left onto busy Canal Street, she stopped pedaling, allowing the wheels to coast on their own as she threaded between cars, street carts, and the hundreds of pedestrians on Chinatown's streets. The air nipped at her knuckles, reminding her she'd need her knit gloves and hat soon.

She wished she'd had a dollar for each time someone called her crazy for riding a bike in Manhattan. There were more deaths of city cyclists than any other accident in New York, well-meaning people said. They never understood. Being perched on the seat of her used bike meant security and control to Michelle. Every muscle in her legs flexed and contracted with the rhythm of her tires along the pavement, a feeling she never quite had while walking on the sidewalk. Mass transit was out of the question for her. She'd never forget how she'd felt like a trapped animal with nowhere to escape the one and only time she rode the subway. Buses were out too, which was why she paid the exorbitant rent for her little Chinatown studio.

Gliding onto Mercer Street, where the smooth city asphalt turned into the original cobblestone streets, was her favorite part of the ride. Every bump she hit as she passed galleries, shops, restaurants, and lofts reminded her of how lucky she was to be living and working in the trendy art district of SoHo. Her tires bounced over the uneven road as she steered into the alley behind the gallery. Her breaks squeaked and she coasted to a stop. Swinging her leg over the bike's frame, she leaned it on the fence while examining her overgrown container garden.

Most of the fruits and vegetables had long been picked, not that there were many in the small assortment of pots and planters Miranda allowed her to keep in the narrow alley. A single red pepper shone bright at the top of one of her staked plants. She twisted it off by the stem and dropped it into her backpack before chaining her bike to the fence. It was the last of the free, fresh additions to her plain iceberg lettuce salad lunches. Pulling the cord that hung around her neck from under her shirt, she found the key belonging to the gallery, stuck it in the old lock, and turned it until she heard a click. Pushing open the door, she entered Miranda's office and studio.

"Morning, sunshine," her friend Cheyenne sang as her heels clicked along the wood floor.

Michelle closed the door and smiled at her friend. "Pink, huh?" Cheyenne's hair glowed like a cotton candy aura around her face.

Cheyenne ran her fingers through her hair. "You like?" She changed her hair color like most women changed their nail polish.

"It's cute, but I still like the purple," Michelle said as she dropped her backpack onto the seat of the desk chair. "I can't believe it's already the last Arts Walk of the season. Any action?"

"Nah, but it's still early. With the summer tourists gone, we'll just get the well-heeled urbanites out for a girls' day later this afternoon after they've downed a few martinis." Cheyenne tipped back her head and made a drinking gesture with an imaginary cocktail. SoHo's Arts

Walk event happened the third Thursday of each month from May through September. Art galleries opened their doors to visitors in hopes of making their somewhat-intimidating spaces more accessible to curious window shoppers. Some served refreshments, while others invited various artists to show their art and chat with potential customers.

Michelle chuckled. She knew the rich girlfriend group type well. There were three kinds of people who frequented SoHo's galleries: tourists, who never bought anything; rich housewives from Manhattan and neighboring Connecticut and New Jersey, who acted as though they were in the market for something but rarely made purchases; and real art lovers, who artists hoped would fall in love with their work. Most of the Arts Walk crowd belonged in the first two categories, but Michelle didn't mind. She loved the extra visibility for her own work, which hung near the window in the gallery.

Like many of her New York City peers, Michelle prayed someone would fall in love with her work, or at least like it enough to make a purchase. But unlike many of her counterparts, Michelle's work was on display in an actual SoHo gallery. Most new artists waited years for an opportunity like it. It was sheer luck she had met Miranda Locke two years ago. Michelle had been almost out of money and had no clue what to do next. In Michelle's eyes, Miranda took pity on her when she walked into Locke Gallery for a job, but as Miranda explained, it was Michelle's work that won her over. "You'll make it big one day, little one" was one of the gallery owner's favorite sayings.

"Any word from Miranda?" Her boss was in Europe on a multicountry art tour, looking for new collections to bring to Locke Gallery. Miranda was more than Michelle's boss. She was her friend, confidante, and the person who had made it possible for Michelle to live and work in New York doing the only thing she'd ever wanted to do. She missed chatting with Miranda on a daily basis and counted the days until her closest friend returned home.

"Not yet, but I'm sure she'll message us later to see how the Arts Walk went."

Michelle nodded and turned to the coffee machine perched on the table in the office. "I need coffee. I'll brew a pot, then meet you up front." She opened the cabinet where the coffee was kept.

"Oh damn. I made the last of it yesterday and forgot to buy more on my way in. But there were some free coffee coupons under the door this morning from that new Primo Java place that opened down the block." Cheyenne pointed to the orange certificates on the table. "If you feel like running over there, grab me a cup too."

Michelle eyed the colorful slips of paper. "Hey, we can't turn down free coffee, now, can we? Let's get a fancy overpriced cup of something sinful. Caramel macchiato, mocha brûlée, what's your poison?"

"Sounds like you know what you're talking about. I'll leave it up to you." Cheyenne waved her hand and headed back to the main gallery, her stilettos clicking along the hardwood floor.

Michelle stuck the certificates in her pocket and followed Cheyenne to the front. "I'll surprise you with something yummy." Extras, like gourmet coffee drinks, weren't in her budget, so it was a rare but appreciated treat. Pushing open the gallery door, she pulled her bun free from the elastic and shook her hair loose as the wind combed through it and whipped the ends along her shoulders. She tucked her chin to her chest and quickened her pace, thankful the coffee shop was on the corner.

The leaves on the lone tree standing tall in the patch of dirt dug into the sidewalk had already begun to change—yet another reminder summer was almost over. She swung open the coffee shop door, and the rich scent of brewed coffee wafted to her nostrils, sending her taste buds into overdrive. The small shop buzzed with activity. She scanned the gleaming floors and freshly painted walls. It seemed the neighborhood approved of the new shop. Patrons with their noses in laptops and tablets took up every available stool, sipping from plastic-lidded cardboard cups at high tables. Shuffling to the back of the line, she stood on her tiptoes and visually followed the long parade of heads in line waiting to place an order. Michelle estimated a twenty-minute wait at least, but she'd make the sacrifice for a free cup of specialty coffee.

"You would've thought this was the only coffee shop in the city," a husky voice said behind her.

Michelle turned and acknowledged the voice with a casual nod while keeping her eyes averted downward. Her glance rested on a pair of black boots—scuffed and broken-in, like old friends. She had a pair just like them. Her gaze trailed to the frayed cuffs of worn jeans and roamed up denim-wrapped muscular legs.

"But I guess I shouldn't complain, since it's a free cup of coffee," the graveled voice continued.

Her gaze made its journey along faded jeans to a certificate identical to the ones she had. His thumbnail caught and released the edge of the card, making a clicking noise. A hint of an intricate tattoo peeking out of his leather jacket sleeve caught her eye. "Me too." Michelle dug the certificates out of her pocket and glanced at the voice's owner. She held her breath for a moment as she scanned his face, starting with a firm mouth outlined with dark stubble that extended past his square jaw. Her gaze roamed to shoulder-length hair that covered one brown eye flecked with green. Realizing he was aware of her stare, she glanced away as heat crept up her neck.

"Those cookies look pretty good, though. I guess corporate America knows what they're doing with these chain restaurants. Send local businesses a few freebies to get them into the shop, then hook them on expensive coffee and baked goods."

Michelle gladly focused on the pastry case so she didn't gawk at the man behind her. She spied her favorite cookie, peanut butter chocolate chip, and licked her lips.

"You work around here?" he asked.

Michelle turned to the stranger again. He closed some of the space between them, leaving her an option to step back. An option she chose not to take. He casually brushed the hair from his eye, revealing a jagged scar above his eyebrow. Her fingers itched to reach up and touch the imperfection that somehow seemed perfect on his face.

His lips curled upward. "You don't have to tell me. Shit. I usually don't chat up strangers." He held up his index finger. "Correction: I usually don't chat up strangers in a coffee line. I chat them up behind the bar. Occupational hazard." He scrubbed his fingers over the scruff on his face.

"I work in a gallery. I take it you're at one of the bars," she said quietly.

"I'm at McAvery's." He tilted his head and smiled. "Ever go there?"

Michelle tried not to stare at the way his lips showcased straight white teeth. He could melt an icicle with his smile. She met his gaze. "No, but I ride past it on my way to work. I love the facade. It's a great building."

He nodded. "It's one of the oldest bars in the city. I'm Hunter, by the way." He placed the certificate in his left hand and offered her his other. "Ride, as in a motorcycle?"

"Michelle. And no, ride as in a bicycle." She slipped her hand into his. The heat of his palm warmed her fingers. His sleeve rode up a corded forearm, revealing more of his tattoo before his sleeve covered it again. The colors and intricate design intrigued her, even though she wasn't sure what it depicted.

"Looks like you're up, Michelle. Pick your poison." Hunter nodded to the counter.

Michelle pulled her hand away and ordered two caramel macchiato coffees with extra whipped cream.

"Anything else, miss," asked the barista.

Her mouth watered as she glanced at the dish of peanut butter chocolate chip cookies in the pastry case and remembered her empty pockets. "Thanks, but just the coffee," she said, pushing the certificates across the counter.

The barista turned to Hunter. "What can I get you?"

"Coffee, black, and…." He turned to Michelle. "What do you recommend?"

Michelle's gaze darted to the plate of her favorites. "I'd get the peanut butter chocolate chip cookie."

Hunter held up two fingers. "Two of those, please."

Michelle collected her drinks, took a sip from one of them, and closed her eyes. The creamy foam warmed her throat.

"That good?" Hunter asked after he passed his voucher and a few dollars to the barista.

"Yeah, really good. Have a nice day." Michelle took another sip and turned toward the door to leave.

"Hold on a sec." He pulled one of the cookies out of the bag and handed it to Michelle. "Thanks for the recommendation."

She shook her head. "Oh, no thanks. Save it for later. I gotta get back to work."

He smiled. "Please take it as a thank you for keeping me company in that long line."

Michelle looked from the cookie to his golden-honey eyes. "Thanks." Reaching for it, her fingers brushed against his, sending a tingle to places in her that hadn't been touched in a long time. She lingered a moment longer than she should have. Glancing at him, she saw a sly smile form on his lips. She took the treat and turned before the heat creeping up her neck became visible on her cheeks.

"See you around." Hunter called.

Michelle pushed the door open and hoped the cool air would restrain the heat building in her belly. Heading in the direction of the gallery, she took a bite of the cookie and savored the sweet and creamy goodness dancing on her tongue. The flavors of her favorite cookie teased her taste buds as she entered the gallery.

"What are you all smiles about? And why are you all flushed?" Cheyenne asked with her hands on her hips.

"I just ate something delicious. Here, I saved you half." She handed her the coffee cup and half the cookie.

Cheyenne took a bite and groaned. "Oh, yeah. This is good. So good. Were they giving these out too?"

"Nope. The guy I talked to while we stood in line bought a couple and gave me one."

Cheyenne held her finger up as she chewed and swallowed. "Hold on. You met a guy?"

"I didn't say I met a guy. You make it sound sordid," Michelle said, swatting her friend's arm. "But, yeah. I guess I did. His name is Hunter, and he works at McAvery's."

Cheyenne's mouth dropped open. "Hunter McAvery?"

Michelle shrugged. "I guess. Why? Do you know him?" It wouldn't surprise her if Cheyenne did. Cheyenne seemed to go out every night. Concerts, clubs, bars—you name it. If there was a party in the city, Cheyenne found it.

"Hunter and his brother, Alex, are always pictured in *The Village Mouth* at the best parties and club openings. Total players. In fact, I heard Miranda and Alex used to be involved for a while. I asked her about it once, but she wouldn't talk about it."

"You read about that in *The Village Mouth*, that weekly gossip rag? No wonder she wouldn't talk about it. It's a bunch of trash."

Cheyenne rolled her eyes. "Did he ask you out?"

Michelle snorted, and her mind wandered to the man with well-worn boots and a eyes she could easily get lost in. "No. We just talked while waiting for our free coffees. End of story." A group of women walked in before Cheyenne could respond. "Here's the first group of gawkers."

The door buzzer continued to sound all day as people entered and left the gallery. Michelle ducked into the office for a quick lunch and to check the gallery's e-mail account when she noticed a message from Miranda.

Hi! I hope the last Arts Walk brings in some business. My cat sitter messaged me and is running late today. If it's not too busy, would one of you run over to my apartment and feed Fuzzy for me?

Michelle smiled. Miranda loved her cat, and it killed her to leave her precious Fuzzy for a month. She tapped a message back and hit send before returning her salad back to the small refrigerator under Miranda's desk. "Chey. Miranda needs one of us to run over and feed Fuzzy. I'll go since it's my lunch break." Michelle called into the gallery as she pulled open the desk drawer and removed the spare set of keys to Miranda's building and apartment.

"No problem. Things have quieted down here. Take your time."

Chapter Two

Hunter sunk his teeth into the cookie as he stepped onto the sidewalk. Hints of salt played with the sweetness of chocolate and combined with the crunch of peanuts. He turned just in time to see the back of Michelle's glossy dark hair blowing in the wind as she faded into the sea of New Yorkers. He almost high-tailed it after her before the crowd completely swallowed up her small frame, but figured the action bordered on stalking. Like the first breath of summer air, Michelle's sincerity and sweet smile instantly brightened his mood. The way her face flushed as she spoke made him smile. New York women didn't blush, at least not the ones in his circles. Most of the women he'd met while working at the bar for the past two years were more interested in being seen at the hot spots than having a conversation, much less a relationship. After a final glance in her direction, he turned the opposite way and headed toward McAvery's.

Stopping to admire the outside facade of McAvery's for a moment, he popped the rest of the cookie into his mouth and chased it down with a swig of coffee. The heavy wooden door swung open, and a delivery boy rolled an empty cart to the sidewalk. Hunter held the door for the kid and stepped onto the familiar, worn, wooden-planked floor as his eyes adjusted to the dim lighting. His brother, Alex, gave him a mock salute from one of the high tables next to a giggling redhead in black spandex. Hunter recognized the high-pitched laugh belonging to Alex's girlfriend, Jacey.

"What took you so long to get a cup of coffee? Ours isn't good enough for you?" Alex joked.

"Tried that new place, Primo Java. The line practically reached out the door. New Yorkers can't pass up a free coffee. They make a great dark roast." Hunter tipped his orange cup to his brother. "Better than ours, and their cookies are killer too."

He shrugged off his jacket and strode to the back of the bar to get ready for the lunch crowd. Thursday's lunch hour usually preceded an even-busier Happy Hour at McAvery's. After two years of working behind the bar, Hunter knew the regulars well and their drinks even better. The local residents and those who worked in the area loved McAvery's personal service. It kept them coming back.

"Did you remember to order the extra Jack Daniels? Jamison's regional sales group is in this week, and they love their JD," Hunter shouted to Alex as he surveyed his stock.

"Shit. I forgot about that." Alex glanced at his watch. "I'll call the order in now, and it'll be here by five. I'll be right back, Jace."

"Actually, I gotta get going." Hunter watched Jacey plant a kiss on Alex's cheek before he walked to his office and closed the door.

However, instead of leaving, she made a beeline toward the bar. "Hey there," Jacey cooed as she hopped onto the stool in front of Hunter. Most days, Jacey made her appearance before the lunchtime crowd filed in, to say hello to Alex before heading to her off-Broadway gig. She never stopped to chat. Jacey had something up her sleeve.

His gaze snapped to her as he counted the bottles of house Chardonnay. "I thought you were off today," Hunter grumbled. He knew more about Jacey's life than he'd wanted to know. She spent so much time at the cramped, two-bedroom apartment he shared with his brother, he wouldn't be surprised if she forwarded her mail to his address.

"I'm working later tonight, but I'm going on a little field trip before. Care to join me?"

He sent her a sidelong glance. "Gotta finish stocking the bar for lunch."

"Didn't you guys just hire a barback for that sorta stuff?" She pointed to the other end of the bar.

Hunter snorted. "Yeah, I guess we did." He nodded to their new hire, Mikey, stacking beer mugs exactly how Hunter instructed. Hunter wasn't crazy about sharing his bar with anyone, but Alex insisted on hiring someone for the grunt work. Glancing back to Jacey, he cocked an eyebrow. "Field trip?"

"I thought you'd like to come to the Arts Walk with me. I need your help with something." She conjured her sweetest smile.

He chuckled. "Arts Walk? I didn't take you for an art connoisseur, Jace."

Jacey squared her shoulders. "Maybe I'm not a fan of fine art, but Alex is, and I want to buy him something for his office. His birthday's next week."

"I know." Hunter gazed past Jacey's shoulders to the closed office door. His big brother kicked and screamed his way to his thirtieth birthday—more like drank and fucked. He doubted a piece of artsy-fartsy art would soften the blow either.

Hunter assessed Jacey as she examined her fingernails. She was Alex's diversion of the month, and from the sounds coming from his brother's room at night, she was a sweet one. However, he doubted she'd last longer than the six weeks Alex averaged per relationship. One thing about Alex, he remained faithful for all of six weeks. He wined and dined one of the many beautiful, single women of New York into thinking they were "the one" until he got bored and dropped them flat with a parting gift. A fist full of cash left his conquests with a small conciliation, but it helped Alex sleep at night, Hunter supposed.

She looked over her shoulder at the office door. "So, are ya coming with me or what?"

Hunter blew out a breath. "You want to take me art shopping? Why don't you take one of your Broadway babe girlfriends?"

"They have no interest in art. Besides, I really want a man's opinion, and who knows Alex better than his little brother?" She flashed him another toothy smile.

Shopping for art with Jacey wasn't Hunter's idea of a good time, but as he tipped back the last of his coffee, his mind flashed to the woman he met earlier. She worked at one of the galleries. Maybe he'd get lucky twice in one day and bump into her during their search. He wiped his hands on a towel. "All right. Meet me outside. I have to let Alex know I'm leaving so he can keep an eye on the bar."

Jacey clapped her hands together and slid off the barstool. "You're the best."

Hunter waited for Jacey to slip out before grabbing his jacket and knocking softly on the office door.

"Yeah?" Hunter recognized Alex's "don't bother me now" tone. He turned the knob and pushed the door while leaning against the frame.

"Oh hey, Hunt. I thought you were the new waitress. She bothers me every few minutes." Alex smiled and thin lines formed on his forehead.

"She tries to bug me too, but I always tell her to go see the boss." He returned the smile.

"Thanks a lot. What's up?"

"I'm running out for a while. Mikey's behind the bar, but you should keep an eye on things anyway. I'll be back before lunch."

"Yeah, sure. Meeting up with Samantha?

"Samantha? No. Why?"

"No reason. She's been in to see you every day this week for lunch, then back for Happy Hour. You left with her a couple nights ago." Alex winked.

Even though Alex enjoyed parading his conquests, Hunter preferred more privacy. "Playing cupid now?" Hunter crossed his arms.

"I'm just watching out for my little brother. You've been keeping to yourself lately. You should be out having a good time."

"Not all McAvery brothers are manwhores, Al."

Alex rose from his desk, stretched, and eyed his brother. "Hey, I'm sowing my oats. You should try it while you're young enough to do it."

Hunter caught Alex's look of concern. "I'm doing fine."

Alex stepped along side Hunter and slapped him lightly on the back. "No, you're not, but that's a conversation for another day. No problem, I'll watch the bar."

A brisk breeze hit Hunter in the face as he met Jacey outside of the bar. Taking a deep breath, crisp air filled his lungs. The change of seasons meant an uptick in business, and tips, as Manhattan residents return from spending weekends in the Hamptons and Fire Island. "Ready?" Hunter didn't wait for Jacey's response before shoving his hands into his jacket pockets and heading toward the handful of blocks known for its posh art galleries and shops.

Jacey kept in step with Hunter's long strides. "Was Alex cool with you leaving the bar for a bit?"

"He's fine with it." Hunter chuckled.

"What's so funny?" Jacey asked.

"He asked if I had a date with one of our regulars."

"That sounds like Alex. He's just worried about ya, you know. He thinks you work too hard. You know what they say about all work and no play?"

Hunter felt the weight of her stare, but he continued walking with his eyes fixed ahead. "Are you calling me dull, Jace?" Hunter asked, attempting to not sound annoyed.

She snorted. "You, dull? Hardly. But you should take a girl and your sexy self out on the town once in a while. I heard you were quite the partier last year."

Hunter couldn't remember most of his actions the year before. He followed Alex's lead and went out practically every night, rarely with the same woman. But unlike Alex, Hunter drank too much, which had landed him in trouble. Most weekends were spent drinking and fucking. It had dulled the memories he'd tried so hard to forget and filled the void that had dug a crater into his gut. He'd been on a direct crash course with disaster until one day he'd had enough of hiding the past in a glass of vodka. Nothing he did made him forget what had happened, no matter how hard he tried.

Rounding the corner, he pushed the dark memories out of his mind and glanced down the rows of shops and art galleries. "Here we are. Lead the way, boss." He held out his palm as an invitation for Jacey to walk ahead.

She stopped at a few windows and peered through the glass. "This one looks interesting. Let's go in," she said, pushing open a colorful door.

Abstract shapes adorned canvases in splashes of different colors. Nothing seemed to match Alex's style, but what did Hunter know? He grinned as Jacey pulled out a pair of glasses and squinted at the small tag attached to each painting. She turned toward him, mouthed "holy shit," and discreetly pointed toward the door. Once outside, she went on and on about the prices of the paintings and how her three-year-old niece could produce the same effect. She chalked it up to an overpriced gallery and led him to the next one.

Hunter rolled his eyes when she reacted the same way. What the hell did she expect? It was SoHo, after all.

Jacey blew a frustrated breath through pursed lips. "I'll have to think of something else for Alex's birthday present."

"I'm sure you'll think of something," he muttered under his breath. Jacey wasn't shy about showing off her *assets*, prancing around the apartment in nothing more than a thong. She'd even propositioned him a few times during her frequent drunken hazes, while rambling about her threesome fantasy. He politely refused, having no interest in sharing a woman with anyone, especially his brother.

Jacey swatted his arm. "I'm not that stupid, Hunter. I know my time is limited with Alex. He's looking to set me loose soon."

She'd hit the nail on the head. Alex's short tenure with women was legendary, and Jacey's time was almost up. Hunter shrugged. "You don't know that."

She turned to him and smiled. "I do and so do you."

Hunter bit back his retort as streaks of rich color on a stark background caught his eye from the other side of the street. "Hold on." Hunter dodged parked cars, a honking taxi, and an ambitious bicycler as his eyes locked on a portrait of a woman's face in the window of a small gallery. Blotches of red, blue, and purple adorned her hair in a fury of hues, but her piercing eyes were the feature that drew him. Something about those eyes stole his breath. Raw emotion bubbled inside his belly. Pain and anger threatened to reappear, like ripping open an old scab. But before the ugliness consumed him, those eyes blanketed his soul with an aura of calmness. Something about those eyes knew him. Knew his grief. Knew his struggles.

The sound of clicking heels along the pavement became louder and faster as Jacey ran to his side. "Are you crazy? You just left me standing on the sidewalk. What the hell are you looking at?"

Hunter looked at the painting for a moment before recognizing the likeness of the woman he'd met earlier that day stared back at him. He cleared his throat. "I like this one. Let's check it out. I have a good feeling about it."

Jacey shrugged and followed him to the weathered entrance, where a buzzer sounded in the distance as he pushed open the door.

"I'll be right with you," a female voice called from the back of the studio. A young woman with pink hair and a smattering of piercings in her eyebrows, lips, and nose appeared. "Welcome to Locke Gallery. I'm Cheyenne. Are you looking for something in particular?"

"That portrait...." Hunter's gaze traveled to the painting of a woman's face he'd seen from the window. Approaching the painting, he examined the details. Even more beautiful up close, he'd never seen anything like it before. Brilliant flashes of color throughout her hair and face disguised an expression of sadness and hurt. A series of smaller paintings of the same woman in different poses flanked the larger canvas. All showed different aspects of her emotional eyes.

Jacey's heels echoed through the narrow gallery and came to a halt alongside of him. "It's beautiful. I often wonder if portraits are of real people or are created by the artist."

"I love that collection. The artist works here," Cheyenne said.

Jacey and Hunter peered at the signature: MR Willis.

"Mr. Willis captures great expressions in his paintings. This woman seems to be special to him," Jacey said, studying the picture.

Cheyenne approached with a playful smile that matched her pink hair. "Actually, miss, it's M.R. Willis, as in Michelle Rachel Willis. These are self-portraits."

Hunter stared at the expression-filled eyes and pointed to the portrait. "Believe it or not, I met her just a little while ago. We stood in line for coffee."

Cheyenne wasn't shy in her visual journey up his body as she crossed her arms. "You're Hunter McAvery. Michelle mentioned she met you today."

Jacey snorted and nudged Hunter in the ribs. "Hunter knows how to make an impression." Jacey peered at the tag next to the smallest portrait. "She's very talented, but these seem to be a little out of my range. I'm looking for a gift for my boyfriend. Unfortunately, I can't pay a lot, though." Jacey whined as though it'd make Cheyenne give her a blue-light special.

Cheyenne glanced at the door. "Michelle had to run an errand, but if leave your number, I'll have her call you. Maybe she has something else that'll work with your budget."

Jacey pulled a business card from her purse and handed it to Cheyenne. "That'll be great. Please let her know I'm very interested." She hooked her arm around Hunter's and they left the gallery. "I think we found our artist."

"Don't get your hopes up, Jace. You probably can't afford her stuff." Hunter turned back to the window for one more look at the eyes that seemed to recognize something in him no one else did.

****

Michelle returned to the gallery after taking care of Fuzzy's needs. While in Miranda's apartment, she snapped a picture of the cat playing with her favorite toy and e-mailed it to Miranda. Michelle considered getting a cat. It'd be nice to have something waiting for her when she returned home each day. But thoughts of smelly kitty litter in her tiny studio apartment and the added cost of cat food convinced her a cat was out of the question. Being alone wasn't so bad—most of the time.

She walked into the gallery from the back to find Cheyenne at the desk entering contact information into the gallery's computer. "Any action while I was with Fuzzy?"

A smile appeared on Cheyenne's face as she continued tapping the keyboard. "A few lookers here and there, and then someone interesting popped in."

Michelle raised her eyebrows. "Someone interesting? Care to share?"

Cheyenne crossed her arms and leaned on the desk. "Well, while you were playing with a cat, Mr. McSexy came in asking about you."

"Mr. Mc who?"

"You must've made some impression on him today. Damn, he's even better looking in person." She sighed.

"Who? What are you talking about?" Michelle knew Cheyenne was teasing her, but the thought of a man coming in to ask about her put her in instant fear mode.

"Hunter McAvery. Who else would it be, unless you chatted up another hottie today." Cheyenne laughed.

"Hunter was here? How did he find me? I didn't tell him where I worked." Michelle's heart began to race. It put her on edge, thinking he went out of his way to find her.

"Don't freak out, Mich. He came in with a woman looking for something specific. He recognized you by your selfies up front. They seemed interested in your collection. The woman gave me her business card and wants you to call. Something about a painting for her boyfriend." Cheyenne handed her a card.

"Boyfriend? Oh." As she let out a breath, disappointment tugged at her belly. Hunter wasn't a stalker or even remotely interested in her. He'd been art shopping with his girlfriend. Michelle glanced at the flimsy card: Jacey Martin, Dancer. She rolled her eyes and nodded. "Great."

"I didn't ask questions, but she said she couldn't pay a lot." The buzzer rang. Cheyenne shrugged and rushed out of the office.

"It figures, my work attracts poor dancers. Why can't it have the same effect on rich debutantes?" Michelle grumbled. However, she wasn't in the position to be picky about a sale. A sale was a sale, and she needed the exposure, not to mention the cash.

She estimated her measly savings would last her another three months. Most of the small inheritance she'd received after her parents were killed in a car accident a few days after her twentieth birthday went toward college tuition. To make matters worse, she'd underestimated the amount of money she'd need as a cushion while making a name for herself in the cutthroat world of art. Some of her peers were backed by rich benefactors or had hefty trust funds. Michelle had neither. But she was grounded and had no grand illusions of fame and wealth. She'd be happy to make enough to pay her rent, monthly expenses, and maybe buy a nice pair of shoes once in a while. Not an easy feat while living in New York, especially since she lived in Manhattan instead of one of the neighboring boroughs, but the close proximity was a necessity, so she had no choice.

Holding the business card, she flicked it with her fingernail and strode to the main floor of the gallery as three young couples walked through the threshold. The women walked in first while the men trailed behind them, looking like they'd prefer to be across town at the Yankee game.

"Welcome to Locke Gallery. Please let me know if I can help you with anything," Michelle said quietly. Dealing with gallery customers wasn't her favorite part of the job. She preferred office duties, like keeping the books and ordering supplies. Strangers put Michelle on guard, but she knew customer relations were part of the business, She had to pitch in and pull her weight while Miranda was away.

The women nodded in acknowledgement and slowly scanned the walls of the gallery. "Oh look!" One of the women squealed and pointed to one of Michelle's self-portraits.

Michelle perked her ears.

"I'd love to do that with my hair, but I don't have the guts," the woman whined.

"It's abstract art, Tracey. No one's hair looks like that," one of the others said before the group giggled. "Come on guys, we'll put you out of your misery and get you a beer."

Michelle watched them file out of the gallery without a good-bye before approaching her collection. She studied each one. Not that she had to. She knew each line, each stroke, each hue intimately. She'd painted the series during a turning point in her life. The paintings signified the moment she started to live again. No one else seemed to notice how special the portraits were, but she did. Selling them at a bargain was out of the question, no matter how much she needed the money. They were special to her. As far as other pieces, they were negotiable. She couldn't afford to turn away a customer.

She moved to the gallery's desk, laid the business card next to the phone, picked up the receiver, and dialed the number.

"Hello?" A cheerful voice answered the phone.

"I'm looking for Jacey. This is Michelle Willis."

"Hi, Michelle. So glad you called. You can paint, girl. Hunter couldn't stop raving about you. I guess you two met at the new coffee shop earlier today," Jacey said.

"Um, yeah. Anyway, how can I help you?" She tried to steer her mind from the vision of his denim-clad muscular thighs.

"I want to buy a painting for my boyfriend. He's a bit of an art buff. But I can't afford to spend a lot and was hoping you'd be able to work with me," Jacey blurted out.

Michelle let go of her breath; along with the distant hope Hunter was actually interested in her. She pinched the bridge of her nose. Why would he want her, anyway? Men like Hunter McAvery were seen with vivacious, leggy dancers, not antisocial artists.

"Hello?"

"Oh sorry." Michelle realized Jacey waited for her to say something. "I can't do anything about the price of the self-portraits, but I have other work I can show you. Give me a convenient time that you can come back in, and I'll have everything ready for you to view."

"That'd be great, but is there any way you can bring some samples to the bar where he works? It's not far from the gallery, and we can see how they'd look in his office. Besides, I think Hunter would love to see you again." A giggle sounded from the other end of the phone.

What? It was an odd statement coming from his girlfriend. Michelle was about to give Jacey the "thank you but no thank you" brush-off, but she wasn't in the position to turn down a customer. Her dwindling bank account could use an injection, no matter how small. She let a slow breath out between her teeth before answering. "Sure, I can do that. How about Monday around two?"

Chapter Three

"Guess what?" Jacey bounced onto the barstool.

Hunter, busy filling an order for a table full of barely-of-age women, was in a foul mood before he arrived at work. He woke with the vise of guilt wrapped tight around his chest, and it showed no mercy as the day dragged on. It was the three-year anniversary of the day that changed his life forever. He'd considered taking the day off, but was afraid of a repeat performance of the prior year. Getting trashed and ending up in a stranger's bed was last year's news. Random hookups were his brother's way of dealing with problems, but they weren't Hunter's style, not anymore. It'd been a year since he changed his ways and faced his problems, instead of drinking and fucking them away.

The order of a variety of blender drinks didn't help his outlook. He hated making fruity drinks, and he'd lost the battle to remove frozen daiquiris from the menu at the beginning of the summer. Umbrella drinks didn't fit in at McAvery's. Hunter rolled his eyes. Shamus McAvery was surely rolling over in his grave. No self-respecting Irish bar served fruity drinks decorated with umbrellas. They should be reserved for the touristy chain restaurants in Times Square. Unfortunately, Hunter lost the war on daiquiris. Alex countered the argument by quoting the popularity and huge markup on crushed ice drinks, and the blender kept its spot at the back of the bar.

"Not going on any field trips today, Jace," Hunter grumbled, pushing the blender button.

"You don't have to. She's coming here!" Jacey shouted over the sound of crushing ice.

"Who?"

"The artist, Michelle Willis. She said she'd work with me on a price I can afford. She's bringing some samples over for me to look at today." Jacey checked her watch. "Crap. She'll be here any minute. Alex is still heading out to look at new chairs for the bar this afternoon, right?"

Hunter grunted. "As far as I know. Why don't you ask him?" He gestured over her shoulder to his brother, who stopped at the table of giggling women. The women's volume increased with Alex's arrival, each one touching his arm and giggling in an apparent desire to get his undivided attention.

Alex strode to Jacey's barstool. "Hello, sweetheart. I didn't know you were stopping by today." He cupped Jacey's face and leaned in for a kiss.

"Too bad for your cheering squad back there that I came." Jacey made a show of kissing him back before shooting invisible daggers toward the table of women.

Alex shrugged off her remark. "Since you're here, do you want to join me? I can use another opinion on the chairs. I'll drop you at the theater after."

"Actually, I'm meeting a girlfriend here for lunch, but I'll see you after the show." She slid off the barstool and nudged Alex to the door before it swung open, streaming sunlight into the darkened bar.

A slight form with long dark hair carrying an oversized portfolio bag shuffled in. Looking up, she scanned the bar and met Hunter's stare before averting her eyes to the floor.

Since seeing her face captured in the painting, he noticed things about her that weren't evident when they met at the coffee shop. One thing was for sure; the canvas didn't do her justice. She was beautiful, but not in an obvious way. Hunter couldn't help but try to get her to look his way again, so he could look into eyes the color of blueberries at summertime. But it was more than her features that set her apart from anyone else he'd known. She exhibited a grace and maturity beyond her young years.

"Can I help you with that?" Alex asked as he held the door.

Her gaze moved to Alex, and she shook her head, wisps of hair falling into her eyes. "No, I can manage," she said quietly.

Jacey shooed Alex out of the bar before turning to greet her visitor. "You must be Michelle. I'm Jacey." She extended her hand.

Michelle shifted her bulky portfolio case into her left hand and slipped her right palm into Jacey's, offering her a shy smile.

"Let's sit over there where we can spread out." Jacey pointed to a table across from the bar.

Michelle followed Jacey, laid the portfolio on the surface, and carefully removed the contents. Hunter watched as she treated each sketch, photograph, and small canvas with the care of handling England's crown jewels.

He wiped his hands on a towel and walked around the bar to the table. "Hi, we met yesterday at Primo Java," Hunter said, offering his hand.

Michelle's eyes met his and she extended her hand. "That's right. Hi again."

"That cookie you suggested was amazing. You certainly know your baked goods."

Her gaze drifted from his eyes to his mouth before her cheeks flushed.

Hunter shook her hand and tilted his head, trying to regain her gaze. "You're talented." Her palm was small and warm in his grasp.

"Thanks," she said, pulling her hand away. She turned to the table and straightened one of the sketches as her cheeks turned redder.

Hunter looked over her samples. "You didn't bring pictures of your self-portraits from the gallery."

"No. Um. They seemed to be out of Jacey's price range."

Hunter chuckled. "I think everything is out of Jacey's price range."

Jacey stood and nudged Hunter with her hip. "Look at this one. It's perfect for Alex." She pointed to a rendering of a city pub Michelle painted when she first moved to the city.

Michelle furrowed her brow. "Who's Alex?"

"My boyfriend, silly. I thought I mentioned the painting was for my boyfriend," Jacey said as she flipped through Michelle's sketches.

"You did, but I thought—" Michelle turned to Hunter.

"You thought Hunter was my boyfriend?" Jacey giggled and swatted Hunter on the shoulder. "No, this is for the other McAvery brother, Alex. You and me, Hunt. Imagine that." Jacey winked.

"I'm having a hard time picturing it, Jace." Hunter exaggerated a shudder.

"Hey!" Jacey punched him lightly and turned to Michelle. "I'm not his type, anyway." Jacey's gaze traveled down to Michelle's boot-clad feet and up to her long dark hair, seemingly assessing her as a possible candidate.

Hunter cleared his throat and pointed to the painting. "I know where this is. It's that historic bar on Houston, right?" He bent over the table to get a closer look. The details were perfect. "You painted that? It almost looks like a photograph."

Michelle's face brightened, and she nodded as her eyes met his again. She held his gaze for a second longer before moving her attention to the painting.

"Let's take it into Alex's office and see how it looks." Jacey picked up the canvas and practically skipped to the office door.

Hunter shrugged and pointed his thumb over his shoulder. "Once she gets something in her head, there's no stopping Jacey. Let's humor her."

By the time Hunter and Michelle walked to the office door, Jacey had already moved the table away from the far wall. "I think it'd look great here." She lifted the canvas and slid it up the wall. "What'd ya think?"

Hunter tilted his head and nodded. "I like it."

"I want to see. Come here and hold this, Hunt." Jacey waved.

Hunter strode to the back of the office, wondering how one person had so much energy. Taking the canvas from her, he placed it on the wall.

Jacey moved alongside of Michelle. "Higher…to the left…no, now it's crooked. Go help him, won't you?" She nudged Michelle.

Michelle moved to the other side of the table.

"Get on the table so you can reach," Jacey ordered.

Michelle glanced down, then to Hunter, seeming to question Jacey's request.

"See, I told you. There's no stopping her. You'd better get up there or she'll lift you up herself," Hunter whispered.

Michelle climbed onto the table, knelt on the surface, and reached between Hunters arms. She pushed the right side of the painting up the wall an inch. "How's that?"

"Good, it's straight now. But move it to the left a little."

Hunter slid the painting toward Michelle, the scent of coconut flooding his senses as she flipped her hair over her shoulder. He leaned closer fighting the urge to bury his nose in her silky hair. "I'm sorry about this," he whispered. Her jaw clench before she opened her mouth to say something.

Quick footsteps approached and stopped as Hunter and Michelle turned to face the doorway.

"Alex!" Jacey whined. She blew out a noisy breath.

"I forgot my wall—" Alex's eyes flicked from Jacey to Hunter, then to the painting on the wall. "What are you up to?" he asked, folding his arms and walking into the office.

Jacey pouted. "I wanted to get you something special for your birthday. This is Michelle. She's an artist from one of the galleries."

"Ah, I wondered why you were bringing a portfolio bag into the bar as I left. Seems my brother and girlfriend are hiding something from me. Nice to meet you." Alex offered his hand.

Michelle ducked under Hunter's arm, her hair brushing his skin before she slid off the table. "They were just trying to surprise you. Sorry about standing on your furniture." Michelle's cheeks flushed as she shook Alex's hand.

Alex chuckled. "Don't worry about that." He glanced at the painting. "Wow, this is fantastic. It reminds me of the picture of grandpa Shamus's pub in Ireland, doesn't it, Hunt?"

"Yeah, it's the old bar over on Houston. But it does look a lot like the original McAvery's." Hunter nodded, moved the painting from the wall, and propped it on Alex's desk.

"I knew you'd like that one. I'm gonna buy it for you," Jacey said proudly.

Alex snaked his palm around her waist. "Jace, sweetheart. That's a nice thought, but you don't have to do that." He kissed her cheek and pointed his index finger in the air. "This reminds me of something I've been thinking about doing in the bar." He turned and left the office with Jacey following close behind.

"Welcome to the world according to Alex. I'm almost afraid to know what's on his mind." Hunter gestured toward the door, and Michelle stepped ahead of him as they left the office.

They found Alex and Jacey standing in front of the bare wall at the far end of the bar. Alex held his arms out to the wall and Jacey nodded. "I want a painting right there. A really big one. Like a mural." He held his hands up and turned to Michelle as she approached. "Can you do that?"

Michelle blinked and shifted her gaze from the wall to Alex. "A mural?"

"Yeah. Can you paint it from a picture? Hold on a moment." Alex stuck his index finger up again and walked swiftly to his office, humming along the way.

"Oh shit. He's humming," Hunter's attempt at humor was for Michelle's benefit. She shifted from one foot to another, seemingly uncomfortable. Michelle bit her lower lip as he studied her from the corner of his eye. She wore a thin veil of normalcy, but she seemed out of her comfort zone. Her eyes met his before her gaze darted to the floor.

Alex returned with a photograph. "I want this—" He handed the picture to Michelle. "—there." He pointed at the wall. Hunter looked over Michelle's shoulder. He knew the picture well. It was the original McAvery's Pub in Dublin. Alex always talked about enlarging the photograph and hanging it in the bar.

"Hmm, I'll be honest. I've never done something as big as a mural. I don't know if I could do it. There must be mural artists in the city you can hire," she said, her eyes glued to the picture. "It is a great scene, though."

"I'm sure there are others, but I like your work. I want you to do it. So what do you say?"

"There's no arguing with Alex once he's made up his mind." Hunter chuckled.

"I don't know. It'll take a while, and I have a job at the gallery," Michelle said, glancing up from the picture.

"Where do you work?" Alex asked.

"Locke Gallery on Mercer."

A smile formed on Alex's lips. "You work for Miranda Locke?"

Michelle nodded.

"Small world. I know Miranda."

Jacey tilted her head, raising her eyebrows. "Do you, Alex?"

Alex laughed. "Yes, but I haven't seen her in years. Look, it's no rush. You can work on the mural at the end of your shift at the gallery and on your days off. How does five thousand sound?"

"Five thousand dollars?" Michelle blurted out. She smiled and opened her mouth but closed it again. Considering the offer, she tilted her head. "Seriously?"

Alex chuckled. "I don't kid around about money. You know how much time it'll take. Tell me, do you think it's a fair offer?"

Michelle nodded slowly. "I think it's more than fair."

"Good. So we have a deal?"

Her eyes moved to the blank wall, then to Alex. "I'll have to run it by Miranda first. I open the gallery most days and don't leave until midafternoon."

"You can come after work for a couple hours each day. Our customers will love to watch you create a masterpiece." Alex checked his watch. "Give us a call with your decision. I have to get to my appointment. It was nice to meet you, Michelle. Hope we'll be seeing a lot more of you over the coming weeks." He shook her hand and took a step toward the door before turning around. "Please tell Miranda I say hello."

"I will, but she's away until next month."

Alex seemed relieved. "Good timing, then," he said under his breath.

Jacey followed him. "How do you know this Miranda woman, Alex?"

Hunter chuckled and turned to Michelle. "He can get a little pushy." He tilted his head, his gaze on her bottom lip as she worried the plump flesh between her teeth. "You don't sound too excited about it."

She puffed a breath from her cheeks and moved to the table. Michelle gathered her sketches and canvases into a pile. "It's a very generous offer that I can't afford to turn down. I just have to think about it. I'm not used to painting in front of an audience."

Hunter picked up a canvas from his side of the table and handed it to her. He noticed her shaky hands as she took the painting from him. "The bar is a lot of fun. You'll have a good time here."

Michelle met his gaze. "I'm not a bar person. I don't drink or hang out, so bars aren't fun places for me."

Hunter picked up her portfolio from the floor. "You make hanging out sound like a bad thing. Bars aren't just for drinking. Some people come here and sip on soda and watch a game on TV, grab a bite to eat, or just hang out with friends. McAvery's doesn't get wild and crazy."

"It's just not my scene," she said, offering him a tight smile and sliding her work into the case.

"So, what is your scene?"

Michelle carefully zipped the bag. "I know it's hard for a bartender to understand this, but I don't hang out. I work, and I paint. That's pretty much my life." She shrugged and lifted the strap over her shoulder.

Hunter studied her as he walked her to the door. "You'd be surprised to know that our lives aren't that much different."

She chuckled. "Yeah, right. Please thank Alex again for me and I'll be in touch."

Hunter held the door for Michelle as she hurried out of the bar. He shook his head. "We aren't much different. Not much at all," he muttered to himself, picturing her eyes in the portrait.

****

Michelle squinted into the sunlight and adjusted the portfolio case strap on her shoulder, attempting to act as close to normal as possible. The door closed behind her, and she stopped at the edge of the building. Leaning against the brick wall, she blew out the air she held captive in her lungs and sucked in a new breath through her nose and pushed it out pursed lips.

Five thousand dollars. It was enough to pay her rent through the end of the year, and rebuild her savings with her salary from the gallery. Finally, the break she waited for. She'd actually get paid for her art. Taking the job would possibly open new doors for her if she could just bring herself to do it. The thought of dozens of eyes on her while she worked put her heartbeat into overdrive.

She was happy blending into a crowd and not being the center of attention. What if she couldn't work with people scrutinizing her every stroke?

The built-in audience wasn't her only problem. The thought of working next to Hunter McAvery for the next few weeks unleashed a swarm of butterflies in her belly. The man set her insides on fire. She'd spent the better part of two years avoiding men, especially men as appetizing as Hunter. She'd done a good job of staying away from them or, at the very least, giving them no indication she was interested. Warning bells went off in her head when she stood next to him. A sexy bartender who, according to Cheyenne, had a bad-boy reputation wasn't the best choice for jumping back in the so-called saddle. However, Michelle couldn't ignore the way her heart raced when he looked her way. Everything about him screamed run the other way, but her body begged her to defied logic.

She wanted to examine his tattoo, which she first noticed at the coffee shop. It was the head of a fish. A red koi fish. The design was beautifully detailed. She had to stop herself from imagining unbuttoning the cuff on his long sleeve and pushing up the fabric to reveal the entire piece.

Who was she kidding? If Cheyenne's facts were straight, the McAvery brothers were the quintessential New York playboys. She was sure they spent weekend nights hopping from one party to the next—and one woman's bed to the next. They lived in a world completely different from hers. Michelle rarely ventured beyond her small circle. Her friends could be counted on one hand and still have room to spare. Hunter and Michelle's lives were on opposite ends of the spectrum. But that didn't stop her from wondering if his lips were as soft and sweet as the peanut butter chocolate chip cookie from Primo Java.

Her fingers ran up and down the cold, rough surface of the brick facade. The touch anchored her to the present. But with clarity came the realization that she still had a fear of crowds. The thought of trying to work in a bar filled with people made her chest tighten as though there were invisible arms wrapped around her ribcage, compressing her lungs until she was short of breath. Sucking in as much air as her chest could hold, she let it out quickly to take another. Michelle shook her head slightly and let the city air flow through her lungs freely. *You can do this, Willis. If you want it bad enough, you'll make it work.* She had two choices. She could play it safe and decline the generous offer, or she could take a big step forward with her career.

Tilting her head upward, she focused on the battered McAvery's sign hanging on a bracket. The building stood proud as a landmark South of Houston. Most artists would be thrilled to have the opportunity Michelle had been handed. As she pushed off the wall to return the gallery, she let her mind wander to thoughts of accepting Alex's offer and working at McAvery's for the next few weeks. Her heart beat a little faster as her thoughts turned to Hunter.

Walking back to the gallery, she stopped at the shop window of a well-known photographer, Matteo Torno. His fans paid thousands for one of his prints. And those lucky enough to afford a collection of Torno's work waited months, sometimes years, for his precious numbered prints. She'd read Torno made it big after he won a photography contest. The prize-winning picture hung on display in the Plaza Hotel's lobby. All it took was one lucky break for Torno's success. *The mural commission could be her lucky break*, she thought as she continued toward Locke Gallery.

She spotted Cheyenne's pink hair through the window as her friend anxiously awaited her return. Michelle strode into the gallery and set her portfolio against the desk.

"So? What did she buy? How much? I hope you didn't undercut yourself."

"Hold on, hold on. Take a breath." Michelle laughed. "She didn't buy anything."

Cheyenne's eyes opened wide. "What? Oh, I know. She couldn't afford you. Right?" She folded her arms.

"Not exactly. Her boyfriend walked in and offered me big bucks to paint a mural in his bar."

"Hunter?"

"Not Hunter. Jacey's boyfriend is Hunter's brother, Alex."

"Ah, the other McSexy. You really lucked out. A mural, huh? You're gonna do it, right?"

Michelle ran her fingers through her hair. "I don't know."

"Seriously? Why would you turn it down?"

Michelle held up a finger. "First, I'm not a mural artist. I've never worked on anything that large before." She flipped up her index and middle finger. "Second, I'd have to paint with people watching me. That would totally freak me out. Third, I have a responsibility here, especially with Miranda gone." She held three fingers out and looked at her hand.

Cheyenne grabbed her fingers and tugged her hand until Michelle looked her in the eye. "What's the fourth reason?"

"Why do you think there's another reason?"

"Because the ones you gave me are lame. You know you can paint a mural. It's the same as painting on canvas only bigger. As far as people watching you, just pop in your earbuds like you do when you paint and you won't even notice them. I've got things covered here until Miranda comes back, so if you need to leave a little early to work on the mural, it's no problem. Let's talk about the hot and sexy elephant in the room, which is the real problem, isn't it?"

Michelle pushed away the strands of hair sticking to her suddenly warm cheeks. "The hot and sexy elephant. Nice image, Chey."

"Face it, it's been forever since you've been out with a guy. I can't even imagine when the last time you had sex was."

Michelle rubbed the knot forming next to her shoulder. "I can't believe we're even talking about this."

"That long, huh?"

"I'm not good with men, or with crowds, or in bars. What if I sign on to do this and...." Michelle pinched the bridge of her nose.

"And what?"

"I don't know. That's the thing. I don't know."

"You can't control everything. But you need to get yourself out there and live life. You live in one of the biggest cities in the world, and you can count your friends on one hand. Go. Explore. Live. Paint that mural. You'll kick yourself later if you don't. Or I'll kick you now." Cheyenne winked and lifted her foot.

Michelle swatted her friend on the arm and picked up her portfolio case. Cheyenne was right: she'd regret passing up the opportunity. "I'll e-mail Miranda and see what she says," Michelle said and shuffled to the office. However, she already knew Miranda would think she was crazy not to do it.

Tapping the keyboard to awaken the computer, Michelle glanced at Miranda's painting above the desk. Two bodies intertwined. One with a deep mocha skin tone like Miranda, the other with a contrasting pale hue. The combination was beautiful. Michelle had always wondered who the mystery lover was in the painting. Her thoughts moved to the koi fish tattoo and its owner as she typed a note to her friend.

COLORS OF US

Chapter Four

"Where's that brush?" Michelle scanned the table as she packed her old wooden box with art supplies.

"You only have eighteen gazillion brushes, Mich. Can you be more specific?" Cheyenne asked from behind her.

"You know, the one I like with the sharp angle." She threw her hands up.

"You mean this one?" Cheyenne picked up a brush from Michelle's easel.

Michelle took a deep breath and held the box open for Cheyenne to drop the brush in. Her gaze snapped to Cheyenne. "What am I going to do without you?"

Cheyenne laughed. "I'll be like six blocks away, silly. Someone's got to close the gallery while you're hanging out with the McSexy brothers."

Michelle's cheeks heated. "Stop it with the McSexy stuff, Chey. I won't be able to look them in the eye when I get there." She ran her fingers through her hair. "Seriously, it's really bad timing to do this while Miranda's gone. I should just call Alex back and tell him I can't do it." A ball of guilt lodged in her stomach, and she couldn't stop thinking she was abandoning both of her only friends by taking on the mural. She'd figured she could buy time before the project began, but Alex asked her to start as soon as possible. Something about having it done before their fall fling, whatever that was.

Cheyenne lifted her palm to Michelle. "Stop it. You know Miranda is okay with it. In fact, she sent me a text after she e-mailed you. She said to make sure you didn't back out at the last second. She knows you so well. I hate to tell you, but there's no backing out now.

Anyway, you need the money. Plus, it'll be good for you to get out of the gallery. All you do is work."

"I'll be working there too," Michelle said as she packed her supplies.

"True, but it's a different atmosphere. Take advantage of it and don't close yourself off like you usually do in social situations. I have a feeling this will open a lot of doors for you. Professionally and personally."

"I think you're reading much more into this. So what if Hunter McAvery is incredibly handsome and sweet? Isn't that what bartenders are supposed to be?"

Cheyenne shot her a knowing smile. "I didn't mention Hunter. But you did. You're into him, aren't you? There's hope for you yet." Cheyenne rubbed her hands together the way she always did when she was up to no good.

"I'm not into Hunter. I don't even know him. Besides, he's hardly my type." She shoved a few more items in her bag before zipping it up.

"Why? Because he's fun, doesn't work all day and then sit in his apartment all night like someone else I know," Cheyenne taunted.

"Very funny. He's a partier and a player. You even said it yourself. Alex and Hunter are always in the gossip section of *The Village Mouth*. I'm not about to become a McAvery brother groupie. Anyway, I don't drink, so why would I be interested in a bartender?" But her heart sped up when she thought about his green-flecked eyes. She shook her head. "I'm there to do a job and that's it. Besides, you know I don't have a great track record with men."

Her last date was six months ago. Cheyenne had set her up with a friend of Chey's boyfriend. What a disaster that was.

"One date doesn't make a track record. I wish you'd let me set you up again. Flint has a friend...."

Michelle held up her hand. "No more setups. That was the most awkward night I'd ever had." Michelle adored Chey, but she certainly didn't share her taste in men.

Cheyenne laughed. "You two had so much in common. I don't get it."

"Um, the way I remember it, the only thing we had in common was a love of pizza. And who doesn't love pizza?"

Both women giggled.

Michelle cocked her head to the side. "Don't feel like you have to worry about me. I'm doing fine. I don't need anyone at this point in my life. Growing my career is what I need to focus on, which is why I agreed to this project. I'm doing well on my own, and that's how I like it now."

Cheyenne reached out and grasped Michelle's shoulders. "Look. You have too much to offer to keep pushing people—okay, men—away. Just keep yourself open to the possibility. That's all I'm asking of you."

"I know, and yes, I will keep the possibility open. But don't hold your breath. Men don't flock to a brooding artist with social issues." Michelle hugged Cheyenne before picking up her worn canvas bag. "I almost forgot these." She grabbed her iPod and earphones from her easel. "Well, I guess that's it. I'm ready to roll."

"Break a leg. Or whatever it is artists do." Cheyenne gave her a last hug before Michelle strapped her bag around her back and opened the door to the alley.

She mounted her bike and glanced over her shoulder. "Considering, I'm about to ride this thing through Manhattan traffic, 'break a leg' is probably not the most appropriate thing to say." She winked and turned toward the street, listening to Cheyenne snicker and close the back door.

****

Alex leaned his elbows on the bar and gestured to Hunter.

"What's up?" Hunter asked, pouring a beer at the tap.

"Michelle is starting the mural today," Alex said, looking at his watch. "She'll be here any minute. I have to talk to you about some ground rules."

"Ground rules?" He placed the beer in front of a customer and turned his back to Alex. His brother was a controlling bastard when he wanted to be. Since their mother's death just before Hunter started college, he'd taken over the role of Hunter's parent. Even though Hunter was twenty-six, Alex still tried to tell him what to do.

"She's off-limits."

Hunter pretended not to hear his brother as he rang up the customer's receipt.

"Hunter, did you hear me?"

Hunter turned around and stared at his brother. "Where the hell is this coming from?"

Alex sat on one of the barstools. "Her boss, Miranda Locke, texted me and said if anything happens to her here, she'll make my life miserable. And believe me, she can do it."

Hunter placed his palms on the bar's surface. "Help me understand how that translates into Michelle being 'off-limits,' as you say."

"All I'm saying is that you keep it at a professional level whiles she's working on the mural. I don't need any drama, and I sure as hell don't need to feel the wrath of Miranda Locke."

Hunter narrowed his eyes and shook his head. "First of all, I'm always professional with the staff and customers, so this line of conversation is over. How do you know Miranda Locke anyway? And since when does a woman have such a hold on you?"

"Miranda and I go way back. We dated a long time ago. You were still in college, so you never met her. It didn't end well."

"What a surprise." Hunter rolled his eyes. Alex was working his last nerve.

"She doesn't have a hold on me. I'm just trying to fend off any issues. So, we have a deal?"

Hunter opened his mouth to tell Alex exactly what he thought of his "ground rules" when the door opened.

A few leaves blew in as Michelle appeared in the open doorway. Her gaze darted between both brothers. "Sorry, I should've mentioned it before. I have my bike with me. Is there a spot on the other side of the building where I can chain it up?"

Alex moved to the door and held it open. "Bring it in. We'll find a place for it."

"Are you sure?"

"No problem. Hunter, show Michelle where she can keep it," Alex called.

Hunter gestured with his hand, and Michelle pushed her bike inside. She tucked a wayward strand of hair behind her ear as she juggled her bag and bike.

"Need any help?" Hunter walked around the bar and reached for the handlebars.

"I got it. Just tell me where I can leave it," she said, and a rosy glow colored her cheeks.

He pointed to the blank wall dedicated for the mural. "There's a hallway on the other side of the wall.

Nothing there but the bathrooms. You can leave it at the end."

"Thank you." Michelle nodded and guided her bike to the location before returning to the bar area. She scanned the blank wall as she lifted the strap of her bag over her head and set it on the floor.

"Ready to get started?" Alex asked.

"Definitely. I'm always excited to start a new project. Is it all right if I set up my things in the corner here?" She pointed behind a line of barstools.

"Sure, set up anywhere you'd like. And I have your first payment in my office. I'll bring it out to you before you get started."

Michelle shook her head. "Like I said on the phone. You can wait until the end to pay me."

"Half up front is customary, so I insist on it. I'll be right back." Alex held up his finger and strode to his office.

Michelle opened her bag and removed a paint-splattered folded easel. She began turning the wooden planks and tightening the screws until it stood on its own. Then she unrolled a sketch and placed it on the easel along with the picture Alex had given her last week.

Hunter pointed to the sketch. "May I see?"

Michelle nodded and turned the sketch toward him.

He wiped his hands on a towel and walked to the opening of the bar to get a better look. His eyes moved from the photograph to the sketch. "It looks different from the picture. You extended the scene."

She smiled at the sketch. "I did. I added more tables and people. Plus a few potted plants and other items. There's so much space to work with here." She turned toward the wall. "I think the additional details will create a great line for the eye to follow. I want people to see something different each time they look at it."

"I had a hard time picturing it before, but seeing this—" Hunter pointed at the sketch. "I'm beginning to get an idea. It's going to look great."

Michelle took a deep breath and let it out. "Hope so. I've never worked on something so big before." She scanned the white wall and turned toward Hunter. Their eyes locked for a moment before she looked away.

"Oh, hey, I got you something." Hunter turned and gestured to Mikey. "Hand me that bag there by the register."

Mikey pointed to the orange pastry bag.

"Yup, that one. Thanks." Hunter took the bag from the barback and handed it to Michelle.

She cocked her head, her eyes flitting from his hand to his face. "That's not what I think it is, is it?"

"Take a look."

Michelle took the bag from him and a small smile played at her lips. Her pinkie finger touched him, searing a warm line along his palm. It confirmed what he hoped he hadn't only imagined the first time they touched. The contact of her skin stirred things within his body. She stared at his hand before stepping back and focusing on the pastry bag. The bag crinkled as she opened it and peeked inside.

"A peanut butter chocolate chip cookie. My favorite." The summertime blue of her eyes met his as the corners of her lips quirked to a smile.

"Think of it as a 'Welcome to McAvery's' gift. You have me hooked on them."

Her eyes lit up, and her excitement over something so small as a single cookie made the edges of his lips turn up.

"They are delicious. Thank you." She carefully folded the end of the pastry bag and tucked the wrapped cookie in an outside pocket of her bag as Alex returned with an envelope.

"Here you are," he said, handing the envelope to Michelle. "Hey, that looks great." He leaned forward and stared at the pencil sketch of the mural scene.

"Do you like it? I can change or add to it. We have enough space to do anything, really."

"I love it just the way it is, and I think we should get out of your way so you can get started." Alex raised his eyebrows at Hunter, who returned to his spot on the other side of the bar.

Michelle arranged her area as though she'd done it for years, and he was sure the pre-paint ritual was one she was used to. Once everything was set up to her liking, she popped the pair of earphones she had dangling around her neck into her ears and got to work.

Michelle spent the first day transferring the scene onto the wall in pencil. Even without a brush of color, the sketch came to life. As people entered the bar for a late lunch or drink, they stopped and watched. Everyone wanted to know about McAvery's new artist. Hunter was amazed at how she seemed to block everything out except the task at hand. As bystanders stood behind her while talking and pointing, she never once turned around.

Hunter admired her focus and dedication to something she obviously loved. He only had that type of unwavering concentration when he was at the gym or during a boxing match. It was the one thing in his life he was currently passionate about. Michelle seemed to have that drive and passion he once had for his work until one bad move. One wrong turn changed his life forever. His heart began to race and his gaze settled on a bottle of tequila. It was once his go-to shot when he needed to numb the pain. Instead, he took a break and walked outside for a cigarette, his new vice. It wasn't one he was proud of, but it kept him diverted enough to let the need for a drink pass. His one or two cigarettes a day helped settle his nerves when his thoughts turned to Isabel and the accident.

He leaned against the brick wall and sucked the first drag of smoke into his lungs as he listened to the muffled laughter and voices of the people inside. The buzz increased as the door opened and a small figure walked out.

She rubbed her temples with her index and middle fingers and walked to the edge of the sidewalk. Her shoulders rose and fell as she breathed in and out before turning around. "Oh! I didn't know you were out here," Michelle said, wrapping her arms around herself. The sun had set behind the building across the street, and cool air took over the late-afternoon sky.

Hunter held up his cigarette. "I recently took up a bad habit. Want one?"

Michelle shook her head. "Just came out for some air. It's starting to get crowded in there." She nodded toward the building. "I'm heading home soon."

Hunter dropped his cigarette and stepped on it. "You know you don't have to leave because we get busy."

"I know. Alex mentioned that too, but I don't like to ride my bike at night."

"Do you have a long ride home?"

"It's just a few blocks. I'm in Chinatown."

Hunter nodded. Usually, he reveled in his time alone during breaks, but suddenly all he wanted was to keep her talking. "You work fast. It looks like you have most of the scene already sketched out."

"Almost. It's just a basic line drawing. The details will come out as I start applying color."

"Well, you're a big hit with our customers. Alex loved answering questions and showing off the picture. I bet he's hoping it'll even help business. They'll be coming back every day to see the progress."

"Maybe you should charge admission." She laughed, leaned against the wall next to him, and stared at the roofline of the building across the street. "I love this time of day. When the sun sets behind the buildings of the city. It casts a golden light on everything for just a few moments. It's magical," she said quietly.

"Spoken like a true artist. I bet you find beauty in rat-infested sewers too."

"I wouldn't go that far." She laughed and tucked a lock of hair over her ear.

"I see you like to tune everyone out." He pointed to the headphone wires hanging off her shoulder.

"I learned it from painting in college. The students usually played dance music in the studio and it wasn't my thing, so I popped in my headphones and listened to my own stuff. It helped me focus and not allow external factors influence what I'm about to do. Plus, if I stopped to answer every question, I'd never get anything done." She chuckled and gave him a sideways glance. "I guess that's a lot different from your job, huh?"

Hunter stuck his hands in his pockets. "In the couple of years I've been doing this, I've become pretty good at reading people based on their actions. I know when someone wants company and when someone wants to be left to their own thoughts. I try to give them what they want and make them feel good when they leave."

"I'm sure you're good at what you do." She took a breath to continue but turned to look toward the sky again. "It's getting dark. I'd better go."

"I can call you a cab and you can leave your bike here overnight," Hunter said, holding the door for her.

"I'll be fine if I leave now."

She headed to her workspace and quickly packed her things. "Is it okay if I leave my easel there in the corner?" Michelle asked as Hunter walked back behind the bar.

"No problem. We'll see you tomorrow?"

Michelle nodded once. "Tomorrow." She collected her bike and offered Hunter a small wave before pushing her bike out the front door.

Throughout the night, Hunter found himself gazing at the lines of the sketch Michelle had drawn on the wall earlier that day. He'd never met someone with that type of talent. She was far from ordinary, and she had a spark and fire that she was almost afraid to show. She seemed to carry the weight of the world on her shoulders. Everything about Michelle Willis was a mystery. But there were clues in her work, from the way she drew a scene by hand to the haunting self-portraits he couldn't seem to get out of his mind. Her art left an imprint on him. It called to him. It made him want to get to know what made her tick, what made her happy, and what scared the hell out of her, because something did. He was sure of it. He could see it in the way she carried herself, no matter how hard she tried to hide it.

She was a puzzle he wanted to solve. The more they talked, the more questions he had, like what she listened to while she worked. Hard rock, country, classical, alternative? His guess was as good as anyone else's. Michelle was intriguing to say the least. Alex could take his "ground rules" and shove them up his ass. He was tired of cleaning up after Alex's indiscretions. Hunter shouldn't have to suffer just because his brother pissed off yet another one of his conquests. In fact, the thought of defying Alex's "ground rules" only piqued his curiosity even more.

Chapter Five

Like clockwork, Michelle walked her bike into the bar and parked it in the hallway shortly after the lunchtime rush each day. She'd made more progress than Hunter expected in almost a week. The entire scene came to life from the lines of her pencil sketch. Before leaving the night before, she'd asked if she could come in early the next day because she'd had the day off at the gallery. It was the height of the Friday lunch crowd when she entered McAvery's.

"No bike today?" Hunter called from behind the bar.

She shook her head and made her way to the mural. Hunter cleared the empty glasses from the bar and glanced at Michelle. Instead of going about the ritual of laying out her supplies, she stood in front of the wall with the strap of her bag still across her shoulder.

"Anything wrong?" Hunter asked, wiping his hands on a towel and striding to the opening in the bar to stand alongside Michelle.

"Huh?" She seemed to just take notice of his question. "No. Nothing's wrong. I'm just kind of surprised," she said. Her eyes scanned the sketch on the wall.

"Surprised?"

"Yeah. This may sound stupid, but until this point, I wasn't sure if I could pull this off, to be honest. I still have Alex's check." She patted the pocket of her canvas bag. "I figured if it didn't turn out how I wanted it to, I'd offer to paint over it and return his check. But, you know what? I think I can do this." She nodded and a grin formed on her lips.

Hunter chuckled.

Michelle turned toward him, and a strand of dark hair fell over her eye. "Are you laughing at me?"

His fingers itched to brush the lock of hair from her face and tuck it over her ear. "I'm laughing because this city is filled with people who think they can accomplish grand things. They talk about how they're going to make millions in the stock market, or get the lead in a Broadway play, or get a record deal, or write a bestseller. I hear it in one form or another everyday. But almost all of them never actually do it. They simply talk about it. You, on the other hand, don't talk about it. You just do it. Then you're surprised it actually worked." Hunter pulled his gaze from her and studied the wall. "You're very talented. Don't be so hard on yourself."

She lifted the strap from her shoulder and placed her bag next to her easel. "You're just using your feel-good bartender magic on me."

He caught a flash of pink creeping into her cheeks before she knelt and unpacked her bag. "No magic necessary. It's the truth." Hunter couldn't help himself. He reached out and smoothed the pad of his index finger along her brow, brushing the strand from her eye before heading back to his spot behind the bar.

A familiar voice called his name. Closing his eyes for a moment, he braced himself for the onslaught of Samantha Cummings. The blonde practically glided to the bar from the front door like she was a contestant in a beauty pageant, her sunglasses still perched on her turned-up nose. Her tanned complexion reminded him she'd been away for the past week. A work conference in Bermuda, or was it the Bahamas? He usually only half listened to her nonstop rambling.

"Hey there, Hunter. Miss me?" Samantha slid into her usual barstool and waved her manicured fingers at him.

Alex wasn't the only one to notice her usually daily presence at McAvery's. Samantha worked at an investment firm a block away from the bar and regularly stopped in for lunch. Her persistence got the best of a particularly shitty night and Hunter ended up in her bed—a fact he was not proud of. Had it been a year earlier, she'd have been just his type: blonde, great legs, and a tight ass, compliments of her spin-class addiction. He must've had an overdose of Samantha-types or women like her—they lost their appeal when he gave up drinking.

"Looks like you were hard at work on your tan. Is that what you corporate types do at conferences?" He joked. "What can I get you?" he asked, placing a menu in front of her.

Samantha pouted. "Didn't you miss me?" She waved her hand in his direction. "Of course you did." She pushed aside the menu. "I already know what I want," she said, giving him a wink.

He grabbed the pencil behind his ear. "Shoot."

Samantha laced her fingers together and rested her elbows on the bar. "Doesn't a good bartender know what his customers want?"

Hunter waved his palm toward the bar and smiled politely. "As you can see, I have a lot of customers."

She rolled her eyes. "Fine. I'll have the grilled chicken salad and a skinny frozen margarita."

"Of course you will," Hunter muttered as turned to the computer screen behind him and added her order, which was sent electronically to the kitchen. Hunter looked at the reflection in the mirror above the blender as the crushed ice swirled around the canister to see Samantha checking him out. He salted the rim of her glass and poured the drink.

As he set the glass on a coaster in front of her, she touched his hand. "Now that I'm back, how about a repeat performance," Samantha asked in a hushed voice.

He pulled his hand away. "I make it a rule not to date customers."

"You didn't seem to have a problem with it a few weeks ago."

He leaned in as he handed her silverware wrapped in a cloth napkin and lowered his voice. "Look. I'm sorry about what happened. It shouldn't have. We were both in bad places." He beat himself up over the indiscretion for days. One night she'd returned to the bar at closing, complaining about getting dumped. Convincing him to have a drink with her, one drink became much more than one, and before he knew it, he had his hand up her skirt in the back of a taxi on the way to her apartment. Women like Samantha were like shots of tequila: great for the moment but regrettable the day after.

"Order up," Becky, McAvery's afternoon waitress, called and placed the salad at the end of the bar.

"What's going on?" Samantha unrolled her napkin and pointed the fork at the mural as Hunter served her salad.

Hunter folded his arms and watched as Michelle brushed the first bit of paint on the wall. "Alex commissioned an artist to paint a mural for that eyesore of a blank wall."

Samantha stabbed at her salad. "Do you like the art girl? Is that why you don't want to go out with me? I saw you touch her when I walked in."

Hunter printed her receipt and placed it next to her plate. "Jealousy is ugly, and you are a beautiful girl who deserves way more than I could offer you."

Samantha giggled loudly and flicked her eyes to Michelle. "You're so silly, Hunter," she said as she

SANDRA BUNINO

dropped a few bills on the bar. Samantha hopped off her barstool, flounced to the mural, and tapped Michelle on the shoulder.

Michelle spun around and removed one of her earbuds.

"Sorry to bother you," Samantha said with a saccharine smile. "What you're doing here is, um, cute. I was wondering if you were also available for birthday parties."

Michelle furrowed her brow. "Excuse me?"

"You know, face painting and stuff. My sister is looking for someone for my nephew's party."

"No. Sorry." Michelle turned and stuck the bud back in her ear.

"I'll see you later, Hunter." Samantha twirled around and blew a kiss to Hunter before walking out the door.

The lunch crowd dwindled to a few bar patrons, and Hunter asked Becky to have the chef to make him a burger. "Hey, want anything?" he called to Michelle, whose back was toward him with her earbuds lodged in her ears. He walked toward her and placed his hand at the small of her back.

Michelle jumped, dropped her paint pallet, and yanked the wire of her earphones. "Shit! Don't. Do. That. You scared the crap out of me." She pressed her palm to her chest, taking shallow breaths.

Hunter stepped back and picked up the pallet, which thankfully fell face-up. He stood and handed it to her. "Whoa there, I'm sorry. Just asking what you want for lunch."

She jerked her head to the plastic container next to her easel. "Thanks, but I brought something."

He picked it up and shook it. The plain lettuce made a soft thudding noise in the plastic. "You call this

65

rabbit food lunch? You're at McAvery's bar. You know what we're known for, don't you?"

"Nope. I don't think I do."

"Burgers. Our chef makes the best. Want one?"

Her eyes settled on the plastic container in his hand, and she seemed to consider the alternate tasty option he offered. "Yeah, sure. A burger. Please." Michelle turned and placed the earbuds back into her ears.

Hunter raised his eyebrows. "You want fries?"

She looked over her shoulder. "What's a burger without fries?"

"Good point." He caught Becky's attention and raised two fingers in the air. "Make that two cheeseburger supremes."

Minutes later, Becky said, "Order up, Hunt." She placed two burgers piled high with fries on the bar.

"Hey!" Hunter called toward Michelle. She stood with her back to him, and her ears plugged with earbuds, oblivious to him and her lunch. Hunter wadded up a cocktail napkin and threw it at her head.

Michelle whirled around, paintbrush in hand. In game-show hostess form, Hunter waved his hand over the burger plates, eliciting a grin.

She pulled the buds from her ears, placed the pallet and brush down, and pointed toward the restroom sign, holding up her paint-covered hands. "That looks delicious. Going to wash up."

"Want a beer or something to wash it down?"

"Nah, I have water." She pointed to the paint-covered water bottle and walked to the bathroom.

He wrinkled his nose at the thought of drinking lukewarm water, scooped some ice into a glass and held it under the sink faucet. He added a lemon wedge and placed it next to her plate. He walked around the bar and took a seat on a stool in front of one of the burgers.

Michelle crept around him and reached over to take her plate.

"Aren't you going to sit down and eat?"

She hesitated. "I was going to eat while I worked."

"Suit yourself. But you can't get the full experience a McAvery burger unless you're sitting at the bar." He shrugged, picked up his burger, and sank his teeth into a healthy bite.

She slid onto the stool next to him. Using both hands, she picked up the oversized burger and rested her elbows on the counter. She inhaled deep, savoring the aroma before taking a bite. He turned his face slightly and watched as she chewed slowly with her eyes closed. It was almost sensual. "Mmm." Hunter glanced at the curve of her neck as she swallowed. "Oh, that's amazing. I don't remember the last burger I've had."

"You don't eat meat or something?"

Michelle took a sip of water and made a snorting noise. "I obviously eat meat." She held up the burger. "It's just not in the budget. You know, the whole starving-artist thing." She popped one of the fries in her mouth and smiled while she chewed. "So good," she said, covering her mouth.

"That's why you took this job?" Hunter nodded to the mural. "For the money? You seemed a little hesitant to do it."

Michelle followed his gaze to the wall. "It's not normally something I'd do, but the rent in this city is insane, so sometimes you just have to suck it up. You know? Plus, I love the challenge."

"If money's an issue, why don't you move to one of the boroughs? I'm sure you can get something cheaper."

"I need to be in walking, or at least riding distance, of the gallery. I don't ride mass transit, and if I have to pay taxi fare, I may as well live here."

"So why no bike today."

"Midday is the worst time to ride around here, so I walked," she said before plopping the lemon wedge into her water and stirring it with the straw.

"Let me get this straight. You're a New Yorker and don't ride the subway?"

"Nope."

"Why not?"

Michelle shrugged and took another bite of her burger. Swallowing, she washed it down with a sip of water. "You know, she likes you."

"What? Who?" Hunter turned in surprise at her sudden change in subject.

"The woman who sat here during the lunch hour. She likes you."

"Samantha? Nah." Hunter popped the last bite of his burger in his mouth.

"Yeah. I heard her fawning all over you. I thought you guys love girls like that. All perfect, perky, and blonde."

Hunter leaned back and rested his arm on the back of her chair. "Now we're grouped into one species? Sure, some do. But not all guys go for the Samantha type."

Michelle raised her eyebrows. "You're a single, twenty-something hetero bartender in New York City. That makes you a pretty good catch in most single girls' playbooks. I'm sure you're double-booked every night of the week. What's wrong with Miss Fancy Executive? Not your type?"

He leaned closer, enjoying the spunky side of Michelle. "Stereotype much? I thought you were in your own little world over there with emo music blasting in your ears. How'd you manage to eavesdrop on the bar conversation?"

"I'm an artist. It's my nature to observe interaction. To know what makes people tick. Emo, huh? Do you consider Yo-Yo Ma playing Bach's cello suites emo music? Now who's stereotyping?" Michelle picked up one of the few fries left, but dropped it on the plate and leaned back and pushed her fist into her jean pocket. "I'm stuffed. How much do I owe you?"

Hunter waved his hand and took her plate away. "It's on the house."

"No. Really, I want to pay."

"Until you're done with the mural, you're sort of an employee of McAvery's. Employees eat free. Yo-Yo Ma?"

"Yeah, Yo-Yo Ma."

"You're full of surprises, Ms. Willis."

She smiled. "How so?"

Hunter sat back and pointed to the index finger on his other hand. "First, you dress in black like you're some brooding tough girl, but you're as sweet as sugar and blush when someone pays you a compliment. Second, you ride that bike through the streets of the city like you're in the Tour de France, but you're afraid to take mass transit. Third, you stick those things in your ears to block everything out, and you're listening to Yo-Yo Ma instead of Black Sabath—"

"Hold on, before you continue, who's Black Sabath?" She knotted her brow.

"Really? Never mind. Fourth, you're a young, beautiful, intelligent woman, but it sounds to me like you have virtually no social life."

"Funny, I think I heard you call Samantha beautiful too. You really are a sweet-talker, aren't you?" Michelle sucked the last of her ice water through the straw in her glass. "Is there a five?"

Hunter nodded. "There is a five."

"Let's hear it, Mr. Know-It-All."

He took the glass from her, walked to the other side of the bar, and refilled her water. Adding a fresh wedge of lemon, he placed the glass in front of her. Leaning over the bar so his elbows rested on the surface, he searched her blue eyes. "Fifth, I'd love to spend time with you outside of this place. Even if it's just to get a cup of coffee or go for a walk."

She didn't look away like he thought she would. Instead, she toyed with her straw, sending ice cubes clinking against the glass. "So, what's stopping you?" she whispered.

He scrubbed his hand along his jaw. "You're good. Too good."

She raised her eyebrows. "I don't understand."

"Trust me. You don't want to get wrapped up with me. I'm fucked up."

"Why do you say that?"

"I just am." He stared into her eyes.

They didn't move for a long moment before she looked down. "Maybe I am too," she said quietly.

"Not like me, Michelle. Not like me."

She took a sip of her water and met his gaze once more. "You know what you said to me about being hard on myself? I think you can use that advice too." She tipped her glass to him. "Here's to fucked-up people."

He chuckled and clinked his soda glass with hers.

Michelle's glance fell to his arm. She held her palm out and captured the fingers of his right hand. Warmth transferred from her small hand to his as the index finger of her other hand traced the lines of his tattoo. "May I see the rest?" Her questioning eyes trailed back to meet his. He nodded and unbuttoned his cuff. Her fingers took over as she slowly folded the cuffs of his sleeve once, then twice, until the design was revealed. "It's beautiful and so detailed. Where did you have it done?" The pad of her finger traced the outline of the koi fish that took up much of his forearm. Her touch seared his skin as her heat headed straight to his cock.

Hunter cleared his throat. "I had it done in Chinatown about a year ago."

"The colors are so vivid. Does the fish signify something?" She blinked as her eyes flicked from his arm to his face.

The tattoo meant everything. It was the beginning of the end for him: the end of mourning his loss, the end of binge-drinking, the end of the self-destructive behavior that would have killed him eventually. At first, it helped him muster the strength to just wake up in the morning. Now, he used it as a constant reminder of hope and life. He wanted to tell Michelle everything, but he couldn't bring himself to say the words. Pulling his arm from her touch, he rolled his sleeve over the tattoo and buttoned his cuff. "No. I just liked the design."

"Sorry, I didn't mean to pry." She wadded up her napkin and placed it on her dish. "I should get back to work. Can I take these to the kitchen?" she asked, pointing to the dishes.

"I've got them."

Michelle slid off her stool. "Thanks again for the burger."

"Hey."

Michelle turned her head but didn't look him in the eye.

"You weren't prying. The tattoo helps me remember the people I've lost and it reminds me how much less fucked up I am today than I was a year ago."

Michelle stood still for a moment. Her chest rose and fell a few times before her gaze snapped to his. "Believe it or not, I understand. More than you know," she said in almost a whisper.

Hunter stacked their dishes. The clatter echoed through the almost-empty bar. He picked up the plates and strode to the kitchen, while anger bubbled in his chest. Michelle was sweet and innocent, and he was a total ass in return. It was the reason why he couldn't have a normal relationship without guilt, without the damn memories. Entering the kitchen, he was relieved the staff was on break and the room was empty. He dropped the dishes in the sink and twisted the hot water knob on full blast. Placing his hands on the sides of the sink, he watched the steam float upward as he muttered obscenities. Taking a few deep breaths, he shut the water off and turned toward the door when he realized he wasn't alone after all.

"Everything okay, Hunt?" Alex asked.

"Fine. Everything's. Just. Fine." He pushed past his brother and returned to the bar. With earbuds firmly in place and paintbrush in hand, Michelle didn't acknowledge him as he passed. It was just as well. His dark mood wouldn't produce anything worth hearing, and he'd probably make matters worse.

Hunter helped Mikey take inventory and restock the bar in preparation for Happy Hour. It kept him busy, and everything was refilled and exactly where he wanted just before the crowd was due to file in. Friday nights at McAvery's were busy and he expected a steady flow of people in and out of the bar until closing.

"I'm gonna get some air before the crazy starts," he called to Mikey. He didn't like to admit he was taking a smoke break. He hoped to kick the habit before it became just that, a habit. Lighting a cigarette, he leaned against the brick wall and took a long drag. The approaching sounds of clicking heels distracted him from his thoughts.

"Hey there, handsome," a voice purred, sending pleasure mixed with poison down his spine.

"What are you doing here, Sam?" he bit out. His gaze followed a couple, walking hand-in-hand on the other side of the street. A happy couple. Fuck them. Finally, he turned her way.

"I always seem to be in the right place at the right time where you're concerned." Heavily lined eyes stared up at him as her fingernails trailed up his shirt, sending an involuntary shiver through his chest. "Are you cold? I have something to warm you up." Her hand rested on his chest as she reached into the handbag dangling from her shoulder. A silver flash caught his eye.

"A flask? You carry a flask," he said with an angry chuckle. He was anything but amused.

"A girl needs to be prepared in all situations. Like when she comes across a friend who looks like he can use a little TLC." She unscrewed the top. Metal scraping metal filled his ears.

"I don't drink anymore." He cursed the uptick in his breath, a telltale sign that even he didn't believe the statement.

"One little swig won't hurt, Hunter. It just makes everything better. Take a taste." Her red lips turned up into a wicked smile. But instead of offering the flask to him, she tipped it to her mouth and drank. His eyes bore down on her lips, wet with what he knew to be tequila. Leaning against him, her thigh found a place between his legs and against his growing erection. Her glistening bottom lip begged to be sucked as she parted her lips, and her breath warmed his mouth.

"Fuck," he muttered as his hand snaked around her waist. Pulling her into his body, her curves warmed his chest as the cold brick bit into his back. She inched closer between his legs, his now-raging hard-on pressed firmly into her belly through his jeans. He crashed down on her mouth, sucking and licking the liquor from her lips, swiping his tongue along her teeth. The taste of mint mixed with tequila burned his throat and flooded his senses.

A gasp and a dull thud sounded a few feet from him. Breaking the kiss, his gaze snapped to the side. Michelle's small form crouching on the ground, collecting items that had fallen from her bag, sent a knife to his chest. He gently pushed Samantha from him and was at Michelle's side in two long strides. "Let me help you."

"I-I'm sorry. I just—" Pain, or maybe it was embarrassment, pooled in her eyes as her glance moved over his shoulder to Samantha. The muscles in her neck worked down a gulp. "I was just leaving."

"I'll call you a cab. You don't have your bike."

Picking up her bag, she waved her hand in a dismissal of his offer. "No cab necessary. I'll walk. It's not too far."

"I'll walk with you, then."

"No." Her eyes flicked from him and locked on Samantha. He followed her gaze to Samantha's icy-cold stare. Her arms folded in front of her. *What a bitch.* He opened his mouth to speak, but Michelle waved him off.

"I'll be fine." She pulled the strap of her bag tight around her chest. "Good night."

It took every ounce of self control not to follow her and apologize for being an ass, but it was probably best that she knew the truth. His gaze followed her as she crossed the street before he turned toward the door.

"Hunter?" Samantha called.

He swallowed hard and forced himself to look at her. "Go home, Sam," he said, reaching for the doorknob. The cheerful roar of the bar dug a hollow hole in his stomach.

COLORS OF US

Chapter Six

"Stupid," she muttered, and squeezed a pea-sized dot of green paint on her pallet and mixed a touch with the blue blob she'd smeared in the middle. The color was not quite right yet, but her mind wasn't on paint hues. Replaying her bold—for her—actions at the bar, she pinched the bridge of her nose. Damn it, why the hell did she practically throw herself at him? She wanted a better look at the tattoo. The work was incredible, but she'd also loved the opportunity to touch his skin. The connection seeped through her and ignited a low fire in her belly. She'd thought he'd felt it too until she practically fell over him with his hands around that leggy blonde hours later. She let out a frustrated breath. "Stupid," she huffed.

"Who ya calling stupid?" Cheyenne's voice called from the main room of the gallery. The click of heels approached and a halo of bright pink hair appeared in the doorway. "What's going on?" Cheyenne asked.

Michelle's paintbrush, poised between her index and middle finger, held a dab of sapphire oil paint she had mixed to the perfect shade, hoping it'd inspire her to paint. "What makes you think something's going on?" She examined the head of the brush and traced a line on the white canvas.

Cheyenne leaned against the wall and folded her arms. "Okay, spill it, girl."

"Spill what?" Michelle looked at her and blinked.

"You can't fool me. You're in a funk. What is it?"

"Nothing." Michelle shrugged. "I'm just worn out from working so much. I'm thinking about cutting down on the days I spend on the mural. I'm ahead of schedule, so I can take a few days off."

"That's not like you. You're a workaholic. Something happened at McAvery's, didn't it? My guess is it has something to do with the younger McSexy brother." Cheyenne leaned forward and raised her eyebrows.

Michelle dipped her brush into a cup of water, turning the liquid a deep shade of blue. "No. Just tired."

"You're a horrible liar. What happened?"

Michelle stared at the single line on the canvas. "Like I said, nothing. Hunter is exactly what you said he was, Chey. He's a player. He draws you in...makes you feel...special. Then he turns around and cozies up with the next woman who walks through the door in a short skirt and low-cut top. I'm not sure why, but I expected him to be different." Michelle set her brush on the easel to air dry.

"Men are such asses—except for Flint, of course." Cheyenne grinned a goofy smile.

"Of course." Michelle agreed. Cheyenne was pink head over purple heels for her boyfriend. Flint was lanky, pale, and excessively pierced. Michelle had never seen him wear anything but black. He wasn't her type, but as the saying goes, there's a lid for every pot. Flint was the black cast iron lid to Cheyenne's rainbow-tinted pot. Michelle had doubts she'd ever find her perfect lid.

"Listen to me. You're going to keep your schedule at McAvery's and finish that mural. The sooner you get it done, the sooner you'll get a big fat check and Hunter will be history." Cheyenne stressed each demand with a point of her finger.

"Oh crap! The check. I forgot to deposit it." Michelle pulled her canvas bag from behind Miranda's desk, unzipped the front pocket, and removed the folded check.

Cheyenne snatched the check from her hand. "You haven't cashed his deposit yet? What are you waiting for?"

"I wanted to make sure the mural was going to come out okay, so I waited to cash it. I'll stop at the bank on my way to the bar." Securing her bag's strap over her shoulder, she hugged Chey and left through the back door to collect her bike.

"Be careful, Mich." Cheyenne called.

After a quick glance over her shoulder, Michelle offered her a reassuring smile. "Always."

****

"I'm making a bank run." Alex shook the blue bank pouch in his hand as he headed toward the front door.

"Hey, hold on." Hunter strode out from behind the bar. "Let me go. I'm jonesing for a coffee from Primo."

"They really have you hooked. Are you sure they don't add some addictive drugs into their blend?" Alex handed Hunter the bag containing the cash from the day before.

"One of the baristas keeps giving me more free certificates. I guess she wants to make sure I'm thoroughly hooked." The truth was, Hunter didn't want to be at the bar when Michelle arrived. His moment of weakness earned him two days of polite-but-cold treatment from McAvery's resident artist. Each day since she'd walked outside to find his lips on Samantha's, she'd roll her bike into the hallway and got to work on the mural with her earbuds already plugging her ears. He'd tried to get her attention a few times with a wave or smile, but his gestures were unreturned. He wasn't looking forward to another day of her acting like he was invisible. Thankfully, Samantha hadn't been back to the bar, because she as sure as shit wouldn't help matters. He'd managed to piss off two women in the same night. One he couldn't care less about, and one had gotten under his skin. Her tentative touch as she examined his tattoo stayed on his skin and warmed his heart. Unfortunately, the situation proved he was a fucked-up ass. A fact Michelle was better off knowing sooner than later.

"All right, go get your crack." Alex chuckled and turned to the mural. "It's looking great, isn't it? Glad I thought of it."

Hunter scanned the scene. Michelle had made quick progress in almost two weeks. Not that he had any idea how much time a mural took to complete. "Yeah, it was a good idea. Michelle's doing a great job." Her name on his lips reminded Hunter she was due to walk through the door any second. "I'm gonna go."

Hunter tucked the pouch under his arm and headed down the sidewalk to the bank a couple blocks away. Wind blew cool needles against his cheeks, but the sun peeked through the building tops. Hunter pushed through the glass revolving doors of the bank, his eyes settling on the long line of people corralled in a zigzag pattern by red rope. As he shuffled to the end, his gaze fell on the back of a familiar form carrying a canvas bag. He'd stared enough at the back of her glossy dark hair to know exactly who stood a few feet from him. The line shuffled along and she turned the corner, facing his direction with a folded slip of paper in her hand. A grin crossed his lips, and it was his chance to melt her icy standoff. "Glad to see you're finally depositing that."

Michelle looked up, their eyes meeting. Hers flashed a ray of warmth before frosting over into an icy-blue stare. "Yeah, I figured it was time."

The line moved forward, sending him around the corner so her back faced him once again. Hunter's gaze flicked from her to the counter. Turning to the older lady behind him, he plastered a toothy grin on his face. "Excuse me, ma'am? Would you mind holding my spot for a moment?"

She looked him up and down. "Of course, dear."

"Thank you. Be right back." He proceeded to excuse his way to the front. Michelle faced the counter, but he caught her sideways glances in his direction.

"What are you doing?" she whispered when he finally reached her spot in line.

"I need to talk to you."

"I'll be at the bar in a few minutes."

"Yeah, ignoring me like you have the past couple of days. Please wait for me?"

"I wasn't ignoring you," Michelle said quietly, inching her way to the front of the line.

"Please? Just hear me out?"

A spot at the counter freed up, and she took a step forward but stopped and turned her head and met his gaze. "My bike's chained to the tree outside. I'll wait for you there."

Hunter smiled and returned to the woman who held an empty space in line for him. The only thing slower than the line was the teller who counted his deposit. His tapping on the counter seemed to slow the process, so he stared at the glass door instead, hoping Michelle didn't give up on him and ride away. The teller finally slid his pouch and receipt through the slot, and Hunter raced to the revolving doors, letting out a breath as his gaze rested on her standing on the sidewalk.

"I almost left," she said, pushing her bike in the bar's direction.

"May I?" He reached for the handlebars and she let go, allowing him to push her bike. They walked in silence to the corner.

"So?" she asked.

Hunter gave her a sheepish smile, eliciting a giggle from her.

"What?" she laughed.

"It's good to hear you laugh. You've been pretty, um, serious the past few days."

She faced forward. The light turned green, and she stepped off the sidewalk. "I've been focused on the mural. I'm happy with the way it's coming out. Hope Alex likes it too."

Hunter loved the pride in her eyes. "Alex just said this morning how much he love the mural."

"He did? I hope it's meeting his expectations."

"I think you're exceeding them."

She drew her arms closer about her chest and tucked her chin into her sweatshirt. But Hunter noticed the sweet little grin on her face.

They walked by a few people carrying the now-familiar orange cups, reminding Hunter that Primo Java was on the next corner. "How about a cup of coffee?"

She seemed to consider his offer for a moment before answering. "I'm supposed to be at the bar by now. Don't you need to get back too?"

"Mikey has things covered. How 'bout it? I have a couple more of those free coffee vouchers." He dug his hand into his jeans pocket and pulled out a folded orange square of paper.

Michelle shrugged. "I've never turned down a free cup of coffee."

They approached Primo Java, and Hunter steered the bike to the nearest tree while Michelle pulled the chain from under the seat.

"You know, I really admire you for getting on your bike and cycling through the city each day. I don't know how you fight this traffic." He pointed at the cars and cabs stopped at the light.

"It's really pretty easy. You just blend in with the traffic. Plus, it's the closest thing to running. I love to run but haven't had much opportunity to do it since moving to the city."

"Why not?" he asked, opening the door to Primo Java and following Michelle into the shop filled with a rich coffee aroma.

Michelle breathed deep. "Don't you love the smell of coffee?"

He chuckled and walked to the counter. The shop wasn't as crowded as it was during the grand-opening week. "Apparently not as much as you do. Pick your poison."

"Grande skim latte with a sprinkle of nutmeg, please," Michelle ordered.

"Make that two and one of those." He pointed at the peanut butter chocolate chip cookie. "Mind if we share? I'm trying to watch my figure," he said, his palm moved to his stomach.

"Watching your figure, huh? Well, you do have a reputation to keep up."

Hunter handed the certificates and a couple of dollars to the barista. He pointed to an empty table. "Let's sit for a few minutes. What reputation?"

Michelle pulled out one of the chairs and sat as Hunter took the seat on the other side of the table. "You know, the 'sexy bartender with a killer tat' rep. Don't pretend you haven't noticed the Hunter McAvery Happy Hour Fan Club?"

"Did you call me sexy?" He laughed as he split the cookie and handed her half.

Her cheeks flushed. "Don't let it go to your head. I love the fish." She pointed at his right arm and popped a piece of the cookie in her mouth. She held her finger up and closed her eyes for a moment. "Oh man, these cookies keep getting better."

"They do and you're wrong, by the way. Alex is the one with the rep. I'm pretty much a loner these days." Hunter took a hearty bite of his half of cookie.

Michelle snorted. "You didn't seem too lonely the other night."

"Ah, the thing with Samantha. Weak moment on my part."

"You don't owe me an excuse." Michelle dropped the rest of her cookie on a napkin and pushed it away.

"Actually, I do. If you'd allow me to explain."

Michelle shrugged. "Go ahead."

Hunter rested his arms on the table and leaned in, holding her gaze. "I used to go out every night. Bars, parties, clubs. It was easier than sitting at home and thinking. I drank. A lot. Too much, actually. It got out of control. I decided to give up booze and everything that went along with it about a year ago. The other night I was feeling sorry for myself and, well, I'm not going to make excuses, but I slipped and I'm not proud of it. Samantha is not for me."

Twirling a wooden stirrer in the froth of her latte, she lifted the mug and took a sip. She placed it on the table. "You didn't have to explain. Anyway, I wouldn't know about the party lifestyle. I live a dull life in comparison. Not much except working and painting, but I like it that way."

"So, work and paint. That's it? What about boyfriends?" He raised his eyebrows.

"Cheyenne was right to warn me about you." She waved the stirrer at him.

Crossing his arms, he cocked his head. "Why is it you never answer a question?"

Michelle took another sip of her coffee. A dab of foam sat on her upper lip for a moment before she licked it away. Resting her elbows on the edge of the table, her summer blue eyes iced over. "Let's just say I don't do relationships well. Men don't really understand my crazy artist nuances."

"Nuances?"

"Yeah, it's a nice way to say issues. I have a lot of them, and most people run the opposite way from me. Especially guys. But it's fine. I'm probably better off alone. It helps me be a better artist."

"I think that's a cop-out."

She shrugged. "Maybe, but it's the same thing you're doing. It's easier to get involved with someone like Samantha because you know it'll remain at a physical level. No chance of getting too close. See? Same thing."

Hunter tried to swallow the bit of cookie in his mouth, but a lump in his throat replaced every last bit of moisture. He coughed and slurped the hot coffee, burning his tongue as he washed the cookie down.

"Did I hit a nerve?" she asked, stifling a laugh.

Hunter wiped his mouth with a napkin and coughed again. "You seem pretty confident in your analysis. Am I that transparent?"

"To me, yes. But don't worry. I'm sure you have everyone else fooled." Michelle tipped back the last of her latte and pointed to the door.

With a quick nod, he pushed the chair from the table before she could continue her analysis. Michelle didn't just hit a nerve, she split it wide open and left it exposed. She'd figured him out even before he understood his self-destructive actions, and it threw him into a tailspin. His immediate instinct was to put distance between him and the artist who crept into his life and forced him to take a good look at the shell of a man he'd become. However, Michelle gave him something he'd lost when his world came crashing down that warm October day. Hope. It slowly seeped back into his veins and pumped through his body, healing the broken pieces.

"Hey," he said in almost a whisper as he followed her to the door.

She swung her head to the side, the ends of her dark hair skimming her shoulders. "Yeah?"

"I like your nuances."

Blue eyes flashed and crinkled at the corners as a small grin played on her lips. "I kinda like yours too."

A gust of wind blew Michelle's hair into a dark halo around her head as she unchained her bike from the tree. Hunter's fingers gripped the cold handlebars as the wheels clicked softly. They walked in comfortable silence as the McAvery's sign came into view.

"It must be nice to have a family history. To have a place where you're always accepted," Michelle said, nodding to the sign.

Hunter stared at it and blinked. "I never wanted to take over the family business. It was Alex's dream. He loves the bar. I don't plan to be working here much longer."

Michelle gripped the brass handle, the wooden door squeaked as she pulled it open, and her eyes flicked to meet his. "So, what's your dream?"

Hunter paused in the doorway, his eyes scanning the familiarity of McAvery's. "Not this," he said before pushing the bike inside.

Chapter Seven

Michelle's icy standoff lifted after they found common ground over that peanut butter chocolate chip cookie. Hunter counted down the hours until she pushed her bike into the bar each day. Michelle made him feel almost normal. He couldn't deny the fact that he wanted her so much it scared him. He'd never act on it and not because of Alex's fucking "ground rules". Quite simply, nothing good would come of it, and he'd hurt her in the end. Since he'd rather die than hurt Michelle, he learned to curb the molten-hot desire bubbling inside his gut. But that didn't stop him from staring at the strip of skin that peeked out from the bottom of her shirt as she reached for the top of the mural. When his fingers itched to discover how soft her skin would feel under his touch, he scrubbed beer mugs. He'd bet a million bucks McAvery's had the cleanest mugs on Broome Street.

Hunter filled one of his ultraclean mugs with ice and water. He added a lemon wedge and carried it around the bar to Michelle. His gaze washed over a finished section of the mural.

"Something wrong?" Michelle pulled the wire from her left ear and stretched her arms.

Hunter handed her the ice water. "No. Not at all. It's just that photograph—" Hunter nodded at the paint-covered copy of the picture clipped to her paint box. "I grew up looking at that picture, and I don't know how to explain it. You're making it come to life."

Michelle glanced at the wall and back to Hunter. A slow smile crossed her face. "It may sound silly, but the people I paint become real to me. I give each person a story in my head. It's the only way I can capture a real expression. I have to know what each is thinking. What drives them and makes them tick."

Michelle's self-portrait flashed in his mind as he searched her crystal-blue eyes.

Breaking their stare, she turned toward the mural. "For example—" She pointed her paint-splattered index finger. "The couple over there is on their first date. He's trying to be on his best behavior, because he can't believe how lucky he is to be out with such a beautiful woman. She's loving the attention but glances at her watch because she has another date later that night."

Hunter raised his eyebrow "She's double-booked, huh?"

A giggle erupted from her lips and she rolled her eyes. "Yeah, she's one of those."

He pointed to another table in the scene. "What about those two?"

"Them?" His gaze trailed to her bottom lip as she tapped the end of paintbrush on the plump flesh. A blush rose from her neck and flushed her cheeks. "They met recently and share a love of peanut butter chocolate chip cookies."

"I like those two."

"Me too," Michelle said, turning toward Hunter. Her thick lashes lowered a moment before her gaze snapped to his.

A crack of thunder echoed through the bar as the door opened and Alex hurried in. "Made it just in time. We're in for a storm."

"Damn. I wanted to leave before the rain hit." Michelle winced at the second crack of thunder.

Hunter followed her glance to the window. "Why not cab it home and come back for your bike tomorrow?"

"I'm prepared for rain." She fished around her bag and pulled out a pop-up umbrella. "I'll leave my bike here if it's okay."

"Nonsense. I'll call you a cab," Alex said, walking to his office.

"No. Really, it's not that far."

"If it's about the money, I've got it," Hunter said quietly so Alex didn't hear.

"It's not the first time this has happened. I can take care of myself," she said as she rooted around in her bag and pulled out a silver cylinder.

"What do you have there?"

"What, this?" She held the small canister out so the nozzle pointed at him. "It's mace. I carry it with me to be safe."

Hunter held his hand out and shifted out of the line of fire. "Whoa. Don't point that thing at me. Are you nuts? It's six thirty on a Sunday night in the rain—doesn't seem to me it's prime mugging time."

Michelle's glance moved from the container to his face with an expression he couldn't quite read but had seen before. He'd seen it staring back at him from the portrait at the gallery. "Nuts? I call it being safe. Nuts are what's out there." She pointed her finger toward the door. "You obviously haven't felt threatened before." She shot an icy glare in his direction. "I have, and I'm not about to be a victim." Her voice shook as tears filled her eyes.

At a loss for words, Hunter stared at her. "Something you want to talk about?"

"There's nothing to talk about. I'll be back for my bike tomorrow." She pulled a hoodie over her head before hurrying toward the door.

****

Michelle pushed open the door with more force than she'd intended and winced when it smacked into the outside brick wall. Her fingers gripped the small umbrella she carried in her bag. She pressed the button and shook the umbrella as it expanded, providing the needed shield for the soaking rain. Tucking her bag tightly under her arm, she grasped the mace container like it was her lifeline. Averting her eyes to the sidewalk, she dodged puddles as she began her long walk home. If she picked up her speed, she just might make it before dark set over the city. One reason she loved living in New York is that it never got really dark. She hated the dark. It had a way of seeping into her head late at night and coaxing feelings of terror and helplessness until she was afraid to move. Just like in her studio apartment, there was always a light on in the city. However, the absence of true darkness never gave her a false sense of security. It just helped her feel a little less vulnerable.

She shook her head to rid herself of the fear that wrapped around her spine like a snake. She had a long walk ahead of her and couldn't afford to freak out just because of a little rain. Mentally counting the precious folded bills and few coins squirreled away in the pocket of her handbag, she determined she had enough for cab fare. Not that she'd be able to summon a cab anyway. New York cabs in a rainstorm were as hard to catch as a school kid at recess, and Michelle's small frame didn't help much. She scanned the street at the yellow cabs zooming by, spraying dirty puddle water everywhere. No, cabs were probably not an option.

Put one foot in front of the other. Somehow the song from the old Christmas special played through her head during times like that exact one. It propelled her ahead, putting distance in front of where she'd been and got her closer to where she was headed. Raindrops played an eerie staccato on the panels of her umbrella as she focused on her footing along the slick sidewalk. Each step bringing her closer to the only place she felt relatively safe. Gripping the mace canister in her left hand, her heartbeat matched the rhythm of her footfalls.

"Hey! Hey!" a deep voice called over the whoosh of the cabs.

Michelle kicked up her walk to a jog, her heartbeat thumped wildly and her throat went dry. *Don't look. Just keep walking.*

"Wait up! Michelle!"

She froze at the sound of her name. Fumbling with the mace cylinder, it slipped from her hands and landed with a *kerplunk*, followed by a quick roll over the curb and into the street. "Shit." She scooted to the edge of the sidewalk and squinted through the driving rain. The metal cylinder, her only defense, was nowhere to be seen.

"Hold on!" The voice came closer.

Her heartbeat raced in her chest. She glanced over her shoulder and was about to run until she saw something familiar. It was her bike. Her glance traveled up to the rider, and she breathed a sigh of relief. "Hunter? What are you doing," she called.

He lifted the fingers of his right hand in a wave. His dark green sweatshirt had turned black from the soaking rain. Pedaling to the curb, he swung his jean-covered leg over the side and walked the bike onto the sidewalk. He blew out a breath, sending water droplets through the air and he wiped a wet sleeve over his eyes. "Hey there, I'm glad I found you. It didn't occur to me that I had no idea which direction you lived. You move fast," he chuckled.

"You scared the crap out of me. What are you doing with my bike?" she asked, catching her breath.

"I figured you can use it to get to work tomorrow, so I thought I'd ride it home for you."

"In the rain? Are you crazy? Those cabbies will run you down without a second thought."

He smiled as raindrops flowed down his face. "I noticed, which is why I'm now walking the bike. How about sharing some of that umbrella real estate?"

"Sorry." She shifted the umbrella to her left hand and held it higher to accommodate his height. "How's that?"

"Thanks. You, um, okay?"

Michelle stared ahead and focused on the streetlights. Her heartbeat had finally returned to normal. "Yeah and I can take it from here." She reached toward the handlebars to claim her bike.

He rolled it out of her reach. "Not a chance. Something's got you spooked, so I'm walking you and your bike home. No questions asked. Besides, you're the one with the umbrella."

She lived a couple blocks away, and she had a feeling nothing she could say to him would change his mind. Turning her head to the side, she smiled as raindrops rolled down his face. "The umbrella's not helping much is it?"

He wiped his face with a wet sleeve. "Not really, but the bright side is, I don't need a shower now."

Michelle laughed out loud. "Here," she said and tugged on his sleeve. "Come closer and you won't get wet."

"I think it's a little late for that." He brushed wet strands of hair from his eyes. "But I'm not complaining." He wrapped his arm around her waist and pulled her close.

Body heat mixed with cool rain proved to be a wonderful combination. The comforting scent of the bar on his shirt as she curled into his arm gave her a sense of protection. Not just from the weather, but also from the unknown that crept into her nightmares. They walked in silence, her teeth chattered as a wicked wind blew raindrops into her face.

"Are you cold?" he asked huskily, squeezing her to his chest.

His voice warmed her to her toes. "I'm okay." She wound her arm around his waist as they jumped over a puddle.

"This is me." She pointed to the door. "Thanks." Once again she reached for the bike, only to have him pick it up.

"See, you got all the way home without spraying someone with mace."

"I couldn't even if I wanted to. I dropped it back there. I'll need to buy another," Michelle said, climbing the stairs leading to the building and unlocking the door.

He quickly followed, easily hoisting the bike frame into one hand and walking into the small entryway. He set it down next to another bike locked to a stand in the corner.

Michelle bent down to run the chain around the frame and an available bar. Clicking the lock into place, she stood and sensed Hunter's warmth over her back.

"What if I told you there was a way to protect yourself without relying on mace?"

Michelle turned to face him and lifted her hands from her sides. "Come on, look at me. How much damage am I going to do to an attacker?"

"You have more fight in you than you know."

"No, I don't." She shook her head.

"You do, you just need some help finding it."

"Help? I've had more help than you can possibly imagine. I'm fine, really. The mace gives me a sense of security."

"Did you ever use it in a real life situation?"

"No, " she said meekly.

"Then how do you know it'll save you? Turn around, let me show you."

Michelle narrowed her eyebrows. "What do you mean?"

"Turn around. Let's pretend you're walking down the sidewalk or even at your front door turning the key in the lock. Pretend you have the mace in your hand."

She shrugged and turned so her back faced him and her right hand held an imaginary canister of mace. "This is silly."

"Don't freak out, but I'm going to grab you from behind."

She braced herself for his touch. Strong arms wrapped around her at her elbows, rendering her mace-holding arm useless. She froze, realizing the mace wouldn't help her in this sort of situation.

"You're small, so an attacker can easily pick you up and carry you off in a New York second." Even though she was restrained, his voice soothed her from panicking. "What would you do in this situation?"

Michelle thought about what she would actually do. Nothing. There was nothing to do. "Scream."

Hunter chuckled and released her. "What else?"

She turned around. "There's nothing else I could do, and you're right. The mace wouldn't have helped me in that situation."

Hunter nodded. "True, but believe it or not, there's a lot you could do. Even with your small size. In fact, your size can even help you."

Michelle sighed. "I doubt that. But thanks for showing me I've been walking around with a false sense of security. Much appreciated." She rolled her eyes and walked to the front door.

"Hey, I didn't do it to piss you off. I just wanted to show you the mace doesn't really help, but I can teach you something that will."

Her shoulders rose and fell a few times before she spoke. "Look, Hunter, remember at the bar when I said I may be as fucked-up as you?"

He nodded.

"Well, I was attacked a few years ago. Nothing happened to me physically. Campus police came before he...." She ran her fingers through her hair, remembering that night. "They came in time. I lived in fear for a long time." She hugged her arms around her chest. "I don't want to be afraid anymore. The mace helped me find the courage to walk home in the dark when needed. I don't know what else to do." She pushed the front door open, hoping he'd leave before the tears filling her eyes escaped down her cheeks.

"I'm sorry," he said. He passed through the doorway as sheets of rain poured down behind him.

"Here, take this." She handed him the handle of the dripping umbrella.

Instead of taking the umbrella, his hand covered hers and he squeezed. "Why don't you do something about it?"

She pulled her hand from his. "What can I possibly do?"

He took his wallet from the front pocket of his jeans and flipped it open. "Meet me here tomorrow morning at eight," he said, handing her a damp business card.

COLORS OF US

Chapter Eight

Michelle almost turned around at least three times on her way, but curiosity got the best of her, and she found herself stepping down a flight of cement stairs to a metal door in need of a paint job. "Max's Gym" is all that appeared on the card, along with an address and phone number. She wasn't sure what she'd expected. Her best guess was a gym filled with weight and cardio machines and maybe some spin classes. What she found when she opened the basement-level door was anything but typical of a city gym. The aroma reminiscent of a high school locker room flooded her nose immediately. Her eyes adjusted to the dim light as she scanned the dusty room. Two boxing rings and an assortment of punching bags dangled from stands, walls, and the ceiling. Stony glances in her direction from the few men in the joint screamed, *You're in the wrong place, sweetheart.*

"You lost?" a gruff female voice asked.

Michelle spun around to face the chipped Formica desk. An older woman with gray-streaked hair pulled into a ponytail offered a warm smile.

"Sorry?"

"Ya look lost," the woman said, leaning her elbows on the desk.

"I'm meeting someone here." Michelle passed her the card.

"Yup, you're in the right place, then. I'm Max." She extended a calloused hand. "Is that the guy you're supposed to meet?" Max jerked her head toward the window.

Michelle turned and caught a flash of Hunter rushing down the stairs with a couple bottles of water and what looked to be black boxing gloves under his arm. A whoosh of cool wind bit her cheeks as he swung open the door.

His lips upturned into a smile when he saw Michelle. "Sorry I'm late. I stopped for water." He jiggled the bottles in his right hand and turned to Max. "Good morning, Maxie. Have you been entertaining my new student?"

Michelle crossed her arms. "Your what?"

"Student. I'm going to show you how to defend yourself."

Between his words, the noise of gloves hitting punching bags, and the pungent smell, nausea rose in her throat. "I-I don't think this is a good idea after all." She rushed past Hunter, pushed open the door, and climbed the stairs to the sidewalk. Stopping, she took a few deep breaths of fresh air. Footsteps sounded behind her.

"Where you going? I thought you wanted to learn to fight?"

She spun around. "Where'd you get that idea? I can't fight. I don't have it in me."

"I think you do. Everybody has the ability to fight. Come back in and give it a shot."

Michelle shifted her weight from one sneaker to the next. Her gaze moved from the gym door to Hunter.

"Trust me on this. It's great therapy. I know what I'm talking about." He held out his hand and raised his brows.

She searched his eyes. The heat of his gaze loosened the knot of anxiety in her belly. She had the feeling he needed to teach her as much as she needed to try. Maybe more.

Michelle nodded and took his hand. "Okay."

She walked back in with him and stopped at Max's desk. "Do you have any gloves Miss Willis may borrow?"

Max ducked under the counter and pulled out a cardboard box of what looked to be discarded equipment. "You should be able to find something here."

Hunter dug through the box and pulled out a matching pair. Michelle examined the gloves and tried to ignore what looked to be dried blood on the cracked leather. She picked the offending objects up between her finger and thumb and followed Hunter to the back of the gym. He dropped his gloves and water bottles on the mat next to a long black bag in the corner.

"Let's get these gloves on," he said, stretching out his hands.

Michelle gave him the gloves and slipped her hands inside the openings. "I don't even want to know what germs are inside these things."

Hunter chuckled and secured the Velcro straps around her wrists. "Okay, first thing you need to know is how to throw a punch. If you do it wrong, you can do some serious damage to your thumb or wrist."

Michelle opened her eyes wide. "That's not something you want to tell someone who uses her hands for a living."

"Don't worry. I won't let that happen." He cupped her right glove into his hands. "Make a fist."

Michelle curled her fingers into a ball, the leather cracked as she squeezed tight.

"Good. Now make sure you keep your thumb around the outside of your fingers and your wrists locked. As long as you remember that, you won't get hurt."

Michelle curled the fingers of both hands into fists.

"Good so far?"

She nodded, her gaze shifting from one gloved hand to the other.

"Hey." He hooked an index finger under her chin, forcing her eyes to meet his. "Did I mention you have to breathe too?"

Michelle searched his honey-colored eyes before letting out the breath she held within her lungs. "I don't know if I can do this."

"I know you can do it. Trust me, okay?" He flashed a warm smile.

Michelle nodded. "Okay."

"Good. Now square up on the bag."

She tilted her head. "Do what?"

"Here, I'll show you." Hunter moved behind her and placed one hand on her hip and the other on her shoulder. "Step closer to the bag," he said softly. His breath tickled the back of her head.

She took a small step forward and Hunter moved closer, his heat blanketing her back.

"Now lock your wrist and throw a punch."

She drew her elbow back and took a swing at the bag, eliciting a soft thud as her glove made contact.

"I know you can do better than that. Pretend the bag is a cabbie who cut you off on Canal Street."

"Okay." Michelle inhaled and hit it with more force.

"Harder."

The third time punch resulted in a respectable thud and the bag even wobbled a little.

"Good. That's a jab. Now keep your elbows high and follow the jab with your other hand. That would be a cross. It's your power punch."

She chuckled. "Power punch. Yeah, right." She followed his directions and applied a few soft punched to the bag. Michelle stepped back and glanced at the sweaty men around her. She felt out of place and ridiculous. "I don't think this is for me."

Hunter stepped in front of her. "That's it? You're just going to give up?"

Michelle pulled at one of the gloves and peered at him. "Give up? I haven't even started."

"Exactly. Show me what you have in you. Show yourself."

"I don't have *any* of this in me," she said, holding her palm out to the line of men methodically jabbing at the row of punching bags.

Hunter closed the gap between them, replacing the dusty air with warmth. His scent, a mixture of city air and soap, filled her head. He paused for a moment before speaking. "I think you have a lot in you." His thumb and forefinger captured her chin and guided her face upward so her gaze met his. "There's a fire waiting to be released inside you. Don't be afraid of it. Let it go."

"I'm tired of being afraid," she whispered.

Hunter cupped her cheek. "Then do something about it."

She furrowed her brows. "You think hitting inanimate objects is doing something about it?"

"It will. Trust me. Do it, damn it. Like this." Hunter dropped his hand from her face and squared his body to the next bag. Curling his right hand into a fist, he punched the bag with his bare knuckles. The chains holding the bag creaked on impact. She watched as his muscles flexed through the punch. "Let's see it, Michelle. Tune everything else out like you do when you paint. It's just you, your fear, and that bag." He pointed to the one in front of her.

Michelle's heart raced and her palms itched to hit something.

"Now."

Michelle took a deep breath, pulling the raw stench of the gym into her lungs. Swallowing hard, she leveled her body to the bag and closed her eyes. Pulling back her elbow, her muscles strained and her body tightened as she threw a punch. Taking a deep breath, she followed with the next and then another. Her legs sprang into the motion as she used the strength of her body to push through her fear. The chain rattled above, and she opened her eyes.

"Good, now pick a spot on the bag and concentrate on it."

She found a place where the threads puckered, showing a hint of the white padding of the casing. She pummeled that spot, alternating her fists. Her shoulders and upper arms burned as she continued. She beat it away. Light replaced dark and her mind stopped its endless race to escape. She was in control. For the first time in years, she had control.

She stopped and stepped back, bending forward. She rested her gloved hands on the front of her thighs and breathed in and out. Hunter's muscular legs appeared into view. She straightened slowly, giving her the opportunity to gaze a trail along the muscles in his body.

"That's what I'm talking about. How do you feel?"

"Good. Better."

"Want to try out some combinations?"

"Yeah," she said as she caught her breath. Resuming her stare at the spot on the bag, Michelle pulled her right elbow back and punched again.

"Try this and remember to use your body and step into the punch." He demonstrated. "Jab, cross, uppercut, uppercut." A succession of perfect punches hit the black bag. Michelle's gaze traced the taut muscles of his arms as they flexed with each punch.

Following his lead, she landed a few good strikes on her bag. The last combination made the bag's chain rattle again. Michelle bounced with excitement.

"I think you're a natural, Willis."

After a few sets, she brushed a sweaty strand of hair from her cheek with her forearm and pointed to the water bottles on the mat. "It's harder than I thought it'd be."

Hunter handed her a bottle. "Boxing has it all. Strength, endurance, cardio, balance. It's a hell of a workout and a great stress reliever." He turned to her and studied her face. "If you ever want to, you know, talk, I'd be happy to listen."

She stared at him for a moment and looked down at her water. "I don't want to be seen as the girl with the problems. That's why I moved to New York, to blend into the scenery. To be that nondescript person you forget the moment she's out of sight. As soon as I unload my issues, I become the girl with issues. Not the girl painting the kick-ass mural at the bar. I'm sure that makes no sense to you. I don't want to be rude, but no, I don't want to talk about it."

"Is that really what you want? To blend? To be forgettable? I hate to break this to you, but you're way too beautiful to be forgettable."

Heat prickled up her neck. No one had ever called her beautiful. Cute, maybe, but not beautiful. "You don't have to say that." She looked forward, took a swig of water and wiped her mouth with the back of her glove. Glancing down, she realized she'd just put her mouth on the filthy borrowed gloves. "Oh, yuck."

Hunter laughed. "I think we'll have to get you your own pair of gloves. Come on, we're not done yet."

Hunter taught her more moves, including a front and sidekick. By the time they were finished, Michelle had the basics down. Hunter handed her another bottle of water as she sat on a bench outside the locker rooms.

"Thanks. I never realized how hard boxing was."

"You're a quick learner. I swear your self-confidence is oozing from your pores."

"No, I think that's just sweat."

Hunter stood and outstretched his hand. "So, do you think you want to come back?"

Energy flowed through her veins and she hadn't felt so strong in a long time. Michelle slipped her fingers into his palm, and he helped her up. "Yeah, I think I'd like to try it again." She dropped the borrowed gloves on the desk on their way out. "Thanks for the loan, Max. I'm going to pick up a pair of my own."

"No problem. I hope to see you here again soon." Max said, her eyes shifting from Michelle to Hunter. "Both of you."

Hunter waved at Max as he held the door for Michelle.

"Have you been going there long?" Michelle pointed her thumb over her shoulder as they headed up the stairs to the sidewalk.

"Since high school. That's when I started boxing. My mother said it would help me concentrate in school. She was right."

"She's a smart lady."

"Was. She died during my senior year of high school."

Michelle's breath caught and she stopped midstep. "My parents died during my senior year too. Car crash."

Hunter put his arm around her shoulder, and they continued walking down the sidewalk. "That sucks. My mother had cancer. Alex took over the bar and made sure I had the funds to go to college."

They stopped at the corner to wait for the light to change. "Alex is a good guy."

Hunter laughed. "You're probably the only woman in the city to think so."

They continued to the next block. "This is my street." She turned to face Hunter. "Thank you for teaching me to box. See you at the bar."

Hunter slid his fingers through his hair. "Hey, I owe you an apology."

"For what?" Michelle asked, narrowing her eyes.

"At the gym, when I asked you if you wanted to talk about anything. I hate it when people ask me questions like that, and I did the same thing to you. Sorry."

Over the years, she became immune to the "Do you want to talk about it" phrase. She nodded slowly, "You get it, don't you?"

"I've told you from the moment we met that we're not so different." He shot her a knowing smile.

Michelle stood on her tiptoes. Resting her hand on his shoulder, she closed the space between them and pressed her lips to his stubbled cheek before moving her mouth to his ear. "You'd better be careful. I could get used to having you around," she whispered before turning and walking in the direction of her apartment. She peeked over her shoulder to see him standing in the same spot, watching her walk away. Licking her lips, and smiled. She'd choose the taste of Hunter over a peanut butter chocolate chip cookie any day of the week.

COLORS OF US

Chapter Nine

"Would you believe my arms are already sore?" Michelle called to Hunter as she rolled her bike into the bar. It was her day off at the gallery, so she arrived before the bar opened for lunch.

He chuckled. "I told you it was a great workout."

"So good that I won't be able to hold the paintbrush over my head today. I think it's a good day to paint the flowerpots," she said after parking her bike in the hallway and rounding the corner to the mural. A flash of pink on her easel caught her eye. "What's that?" she asked.

"I knew you wouldn't get around to buying your own right away, so I picked you up a pair of gloves."

Michelle picked the package off her easel and examined it. "These don't look like boxing gloves."

Hunter wiped his hands and strode to the opening in the back. "They're a different kind. These will protect your knuckles and support your wrists without the bulk of a regular glove. Plus your palms won't sweat as much," he said. He took the package from her hands and pulled out what looked a lot like a fabric bandage, only pink. Very, very pink. The ends dangled to his knees. "They're tricky to put on until you get used to them. Let me show you how to wrap them." He tucked one of the hand wraps under his arm and found the opening of its pair.

Michelle held out her right hand with her palm facing up. A vision of her sweaty-palmed junior prom date slipping a corsage onto her wrist flashed through her mind, and she giggled.

"What's so funny?" He tilted his head as he slid the opening of the wrap over her fingers.

She grinned and warmth spread across her cheeks. "I'm imagining how those old guys at the gym will look at me with my pretty pink hand wraps."

His eyes shifted from her hand to her face. "They'll be jealous and will want a pair of their own."

"Right." They both laughed.

"It was between the black and these. Pink won me over. You can use a little color, Willis." He tugged the wrap into place across her palm.

"I'm a New Yorker. Black is our dress code." Practicality was the real reason for her monochromatic wardrobe. Her budget didn't allow for shopping sprees, so she interchanged her few black and gray separates and completed her look with flats or her treasured black leather boots.

"I think pink is your color. It looks great against your dark hair." Reaching past her shoulder, he curled a lock of her hair between his fingers and tugged gently before letting it fall onto her shoulder.

Meeting his gaze, she smiled. "Thanks." Michelle wasn't used to compliments. It'd been her goal to fade into the crowd and not to call attention to herself. But her self-imposed rules seemed to float away around Hunter McAvery.

Returning her smile, he continued the lesson. "After you slide your hands into the opening, you'll wind the long strap around your fingers and wrist like this." Holding her fingers in his hand, he wound the dangling strap around her palm and over her knuckles. "You want to protect the part of your hand that meets the bag."

He stepped closer as he slipped the strap around the base of her thumb. When he brushed his fingertips against the sensitive area just below the fleshy part of her palm, a shiver shot up her arm and traveled to her belly. His warm breath ghosted her face as he circled the end of the strap around her wrist and secured the Velcro tab. Before she knew it, strong fingers captured her left hand and guided her arm to the warmth between their bodies. She itched to graze her fingers along his muscled chest, capturing his heat with her palm. Her gaze bounced to his neck and stubbled jaw, which clenched as he slid the other wrap over her hand. Slowly wrapping her other wrist, he secured the strap and held both of her gloved hands in his. "Make a fist," he said huskily.

Tightening her hands into a ball, she tucked her thumb around the outside of her fingers like he showed her at the gym.

He squeezed her fists. "They look good. You're a badass."

"A badass in pink."

"Let's see what you got. Show me some upper cuts. Right here." He tapped his abs.

"You want me to hit you?" She giggled.

"Sure. I can take it."

Turning her palms up, she made a fist and alternated soft punches to his belly. His rock-hard belly. Each strike made her aware of how alive he made her feel. The force of impact sent ripples up his tight shirt, awakening the planes of his muscular form. She gulped back the desire to open her fists and run her fingertips along the line of each sculpted muscle.

His hands came to rest on her forearms, halting her movement. The pads of his thumbs stroked the sensitive skin near the inside of her elbow, causing a delicious shiver up her arm. Michelle's eyes met his. The fire brewing in his darkened gaze drew her in. Hunter stepped between her legs, nudging her back against the wall next to the mural. She closed her eyes and choked back a groan. Raising her arms above her, he pinned them against the wall on either side of her head. His scent flooded her senses as she lifted her chin to close the gap between them.

"I'm trying like hell not to kiss you." Hunter straightened his back but didn't loosen his grip on her arms.

Her skin prickled from the nearness of his body, and she let her gaze drift to his lips. "Why?" she whispered.

He blew a slow breath between his teeth. "Nothing good would come of it. I'm not capable of giving or feeling… or offering much to you right now." He shook his head but didn't move from her body.

"I don't believe that." Michelle wriggled her arms from his grasp. Her fingertips lingered on his corded forearms, which flexed under her touch. Easing a trail toward his shoulders, her fingers reminded her of a paintbrush's first dab of color on a fresh canvas. She'd always believed each canvas had a personality of its own, and it was the symphony of the brush, artist, and canvas that created the work of art. She wanted to explore the blank canvas of Hunter McAvery.

She studied his arms, still caging her in. Protecting her. Wanting her. Her eyes met his gaze. He stared at her, unmoving, but a spark burned in his eyes. She held her breath, afraid to break his trance. Her palms smoothed over his shoulders and down his chest, stopping at the center of his ribs. Pushing into the muscles of his chest, she felt the strong beat of his heart on her fingers. "Kiss me, Hunter." Raising her lashes, she dared to look him in the eyes, almost afraid of what she'd see.

"You don't understand. You're too… good." He averted his gaze.

"Maybe you should let me decide what's good for me." She moved closer, his breath burned hot on her face, and he squeezed his eyes closed.

"Michelle...."

Her hands traveled up his chest and rested on the bulk of his strong shoulders. Pulling him in, her breasts molded into his chest and, finally, he crashed his lips down on hers. She met every stroke of his tongue as her fingers raked through the ends of his hair. Moaning into his mouth, she straddled his muscular thigh as warmth flooded her sex. She'd never felt more alive.

His hand grazed her cheek before taking her chin between his thumb and index finger and pulling away from their kiss. He tipped his forehead to hers, his raspy breath hot on her mouth. "Shit."

Michelle widened her eyes. "What?" she whispered.

"You. Me. This can't happen. Not now. Not like this."

"I don't understand," Michelle said slowly.

He opened his mouth to speak when voices and a gust of wind crept between their private interlude. Hunter pulled away and turned toward the entrance. Cool air surrounded Michelle, and she touched her fingertips to her lips, stunned by the heat of one simple kiss.

Alex stepped into the bar with Jacey on his arm. Jacey stopped. Her gaze bounced from Hunter to Michelle. "Looks like we interrupted something. You have such bad timing." Jacey giggled and swatted Alex on the chest while Alex glared at Hunter.

Michelle cleared her throat and rubbed her hands together, realizing she still wore the wraps. She turned toward Hunter, loosened the straps, and rolled them from her fingers. "Um. Thanks for the gloves," she said, stuffing them in her bag on the floor.

"You're welcome." Hunter offered her a smile before returning his brother's angry stare.

"Hunter, can I talk to you in my office?" Alex asked, pointing this thumb over his shoulder.

The tension in the bar was as thick as a Guinness stout. Michelle pulled her phone from the pocket of her bag, found her music app, inserted her earbuds into place, and opened her paint tubes. A breeze tickled the back of her head, and Hunter's scent, which surrounded her just moments before, washed over her, as he passed behind her on his way to Alex's office.

She swallowed a groan when a light tap on her shoulder demanded her attention seconds later. Michelle swung around to find Jacey standing behind her. Michelle pulled at one of the wires, popping the earbud from her ear. "Hi," she said weakly.

"Hi to you," Jacey said and moved beside her. "The mural looks great." She scanned the wall.

"Thanks." Michelle stepped back and examined her work. "I'm happy with the way it's turning out." The women stood in awkward silence. Michelle shifted from one foot to the other.

"Don't fall too hard for him," Jacey said.

Michelle glanced at Jacey from the corner of her eye before focusing on the fresh paint she'd just squeezed onto her pallet. She dabbed her brush into the red blob. "I don't know what you're talking about."

"Come on, Michelle. I know the look of someone who's been thoroughly kissed. You don't know what you're getting yourself into. The McAvery brothers have a way of loving and leaving. They love hard and leave fast. Before you know it, they're onto their next conquest. Don't make the same mistake I did."

Michelle turned and faced Jacey. "Which was what?"

Jacey stared at the mural for a moment before letting out a noisy breath. "I fell in love."

Sunlight flooded the bar when the front door swung open, and two of McAvery's waitresses chattered with each other, oblivious of Hunter as he stormed out of Alex's office and sauntered back to the bar.

"I'll see you later," Jacey said and squeezed Michelle's hand.

Hunter's kiss and Jacey's advice swirled around Michelle's head as she returned the earbud to her ear and turned the volume up.

A shadow cast across the section of wall she'd just painted, and she glanced over her shoulder. Hunter pinned her with his stare as a lock of his hair fell over one eye. She cursed under her breath, recalling his coarse hair sliding between her fingertips. He jerked his thumb toward the door, and she pulled at the wires of her earbuds.

"Can we talk outside?" Hunter asked.

"There's nothing to talk about," she said quietly, her hand poised to stick the earbud back in place.

"Please."

She swallowed hard, her gaze moved to her blunt fingernails, holding the brush, and a vision of Samantha's perfectly manicured hands flashed in her mind. She placed her brush and pallet on the easel. "Give me a minute." What she really needed was a moment to think. She ducked into the women's room and turned the knobs on the sink. Leaning on the cool porcelain with both hands, she looked into the mirror. "How could you be so stupid?" she asked her reflection. Clearly she misinterpreted his hospitality with something more. Taking a deep breath, she washed her hands and headed outside to find Hunter pacing the sidewalk.

He stopped as the door closed behind her. "What happened in there, it shouldn't have happened."

A ball of hurt rolled in her stomach, but she'd be damned if she'd show it. "You're right and I agree. Don't worry, I get it." Her eyes darted to the spot on the brick wall where Hunter kissed Samantha. Who was she kidding to even think he wanted her? "Let's just pretend nothing happened." She turned to go back inside.

"Hold on. I don't think you do get it." Hunter grasped her shoulder, causing her to stop midstep. "Please hear me out." She slowly turned but kept her eyes on the sidewalk. "There's something about you that touches me. I can't explain it." Michelle swallowed hard and lifted her gaze to meet his stare. His eyes bore down on her. "I don't want to hurt you. I mess up every relationship I get into, and I'd rather have you as a friend. God, Michelle, I need a friend right now, and I think you do too."

She searched his eyes, looking for the truth. "Jacey warned me about you. She said you and Alex shouldn't be trusted."

"I'm tired of being grouped in with him. I'm not my brother. I'm not either of them, for that matter." His eyes flashed toward the door, and he blew a slow breath through his teeth before continuing. "But I'm not in a good place right now, and I don't want to bring you down with me." Michelle blinked and watched the anguish roll through his eyes. "I don't want to hurt you. I can't." Pain flashed in his eyes. He was broken. Just like her.

"What happened to you?" she whispered.

"I don't want to bring you into my hell."

"I want to know."

He scrubbed his face. "A couple of years ago, I was the cause of a motorcycle accident. Someone died who was very close to me. The guilt was too much to take. It cost me my job and everything I had."

Michelle blew out a breath. Questions filled her head, but she let him continue.

"For the first time since the accident, I feel halfway normal. Like I want to live, like I want to move on." His eyes met hers. "You make me feel that way."

There was so much she wanted to say but couldn't because it would mean prying open the door holding the shame and guilt she'd worked so hard to keep hidden. "You're right. I think we can both use a friend."

Hunter pulled her into his arms, and she smiled into his chest. "We're still on for the gym, right? I really want to see those pink gloves in action."

She tilted her head, resting her chin on his chest. "I'm looking forward to kicking some ass with those babies."

"Friends?" Hunter asked, tugging a lock of her hair.

"Friends." She winked and pointed to the door. "Now, would you let me get back to work?"

"Ya better get in there before my controlling brother comes out looking for you."

"He's not so bad. Did you say you have another brother?" she asked.

"Yeah, Alex's twin. But he escaped New York a long time ago. We don't hear from him…." He pulled the cigarette pack from his back pocket.

She pinned him with her stare, understanding his loss. Maybe they weren't so different after all.

COLORS OF US

Chapter Ten

Fuck Alex. His brother read him the riot act like he was some irresponsible teenager. Unfortunately, everything he said was true, otherwise Hunter wouldn't have told him to fuck off, which he did anyway. Hurting Michelle was the last thing he wanted to do, but holy hell, he couldn't get their kiss out of his mind. The kiss she asked—no, demanded—of him. She checked shy Michelle at the door, and a sexy vixen was front and center. *Fuck.* The sweet sound of her moan played over and over again in his mind, racing straight to his cock. That kiss ignited a fire inside him that had been extinguished for so long. Too long. Not since Isabel had he felt anything but lust for a woman, and even that was short-lived. He'd had a string of one-night stands that left him cold and feeling more alone until he had enough of that too.

The taste of Michelle's lips stirred a wasp's nest of wicked things he wanted to do with her. Luckily, Alex and Jacey walked in when they did, because Hunter almost lost control, which would've been a mistake. One big, giant mistake. So what did he do instead of telling her he wanted to protect her from the world but also fuck her brains out? He used the other "f" word and said they should be friends. *Fuck. Fuck. Fuck. What. The. Fuck?*

He paced the sidewalk in front of Max's Gym with Primo Java coffee cups in his hands. After an awkward afternoon, he convinced her to meet him for an early workout the next day. Hunter had doubts Michelle would even show. *Shit.* He wouldn't blame her if she didn't. Staring into the dim light of morning, he spotted a bike coming toward him. He let out the breath he didn't realize he held when he recognized the glossy dark hair

117

and lean legs wrapped in black spandex. His gaze trailed up her perfect thighs and his palm itched with the thought of running his hands over her ass. *Down boy*. He took a swig of the still-too-hot coffee, which did nothing for his dick. Damn it, he certainly couldn't walk into a room full of hardcore boxers with a woody in his pants.

She rode onto the sidewalk and dismounted her bike. "Thank God you thought of coffee. I was just asking myself why I wasn't still curled up in bed."

Picturing Michelle in bed with a T-shirt and just-woke-up hair didn't help his current situation.

"If one of those are for me, I'll be your BFF," Michelle said, locking her bike to the railing outside the gym.

Friends. She's your friend. Forcing a chuckle, he handed her one of the cups. "You may not feel that way after the workout."

Michelle took a sip and licked her lips. "Oh, this is good. Bring it on, McAvery," she said and pointed down the stairs.

"After you." He gestured for her walk in front of him as he willed his erection into submission.

The usuals filled the gym. The comforting thud of gloves hitting bags echoed through the room. Max's gym had been his salvation for years. It helped him through high school and his mother's death. Unfortunately, no amount of pounding on a one-hundred-pound bag could chase his current demons away.

"Why don't I ever see any other women come here?" she asked, scanning the gym.

"I can answer that," Max's graveled voice sounded from behind the desk. "We're not glamorous like some of those pickup joints women like to go to. And we don't offer Zumba classes." She snorted.

"I'd love to see this guy in a Zumba class."
Michelle stuck her thumb up and pointed it at Hunter.

"Zumba's for wimps. Let's get a real man's workout in." He brushed his fingers down Michelle's back before pulling away as if her body was a hot flame. He let out a frustrated breath and cleared his throat. "There's a free spot over there by the wall," he said, pointing to an empty heavy bag in the corner of the room.

Michelle moved to the spot and dropped her bag against the wall. She set her coffee on the ground and pulled out her pink hand wraps. She began to wrap them around her left hand as Hunter showed her.

Hunter held out his hand. "May I?"

Her eyes flicked to him. Hurt passed over her expression for a split second before she replaced it with a grin. "No. I practiced last night." Slipping both wraps over her tiny hands, she deftly whipped the ends around her fingers and wrists before securing the Velcro ends. "How's that?"

"Impressive, Willis," he said, reaching for her hands.

She pulled them away from his grasp. Opening and closing her fists a few times, she squared up on the bag and threw a few punches.

Thank God one of them had common sense.
Hunter tried to disconnect his head from his dick. "Good. Now use your feet to leverage more power into your punch. Boxing is not just for your arms. Your whole body must work in unison. It's like a dance," he said, holding the other side of the bag.

Michelle followed direction, using her body's momentum to power her swing. "How do you know so much about boxing, anyway?" she asked between punches.

119

"I started boxing in high school and continued in college. It just stayed with me. It's more challenging to me than lifting weights and it's a great stress reliever."

Michelle bit her lip as she concentrated on the bag. "What was your major, anyway?"

He chuckled. "You're shocked I have a college degree, aren't you?"

"Not shocked at all."

"I have an undergrad degree in Finance and an MBA," he said as he pulled off his sweatshirt and slipped on his own gloves.

"You know what my next question will be."

"Let me see some hooks now. Up and down the bag. You want to know why I'm bartending at the family bar instead of working my way up as some sort of up-and-coming business tycoon on Wall Street?"

She chuckled as she peppered the bag with left and right hooks. "I wouldn't have put it that way, but yes, it makes me wonder why you're not using your degree."

"I won't bring you down with my story. Let's just say it's temporary. My living arrangement too. There's only so long I can stand living and working with Alex."

She halted her punches and stretched her arms over her head. He couldn't stop looking at the strip of skin peeking from beneath her shirt. He swallowed hard when he saw it. "You have a tattoo."

She dropped her hands and smoothed the end of her shirt over her pants. A beautiful smile crossed her lips, followed by a sweet blush along her cheeks. "What? You think you're the only badass here?"

He nodded toward her waist. "Let me see it."

A throaty laugh erupted from Michelle. "I don't think so, McAvery. It's private."

Fuck me. Friends. We're just friends. It quickly became his mantra of the day. His cock had had enough of playing by the rules. He scanned the room, looking for something to divert him from wondering about the design that obviously dipped low on her waist. "The ring is free. Want to learn some moves?" he asked, nodding toward the closest boxing ring.

"Sure. Why not?" She followed Hunter to the ropes and stepped inside with him and walked to the center of the square. Testing the ring's floor, her feet bounced on the mat. "This is pretty cool."

"There are two things you must remember about boxing. One, stay light on your toes, and two, never let your guard down," Hunter explained.

"Got it." Michelle raised her fists, protecting her face like he taught her. She shifted her weight from foot to foot.

"Good. Now block my punches." Hunter started with a few slow punches aimed at her face. Blocking each one, she continued her dance in the center of the ring.

"I'm going to pick it up now." His light punches came faster, and she met each one but she forgot about rule number one. Surprising her, he threw a soft uppercut to her stomach into his routine. His force was light and he only tapped her abs, but she was unable to keep her balance and lost her footing. Hunter caught her before she fell.

"Whoa. See? That's why I said to stay on your toes so you can jump away from unexpected swings." Her body fit his like a well-worn glove. Her curves melded into just the right places. Memories of their kiss flooded his senses. Her scent of coconut and flowers surrounded him, drawing him in. His fingers trailed along her waist and up her back. His erection, now in full glory, nudged at her stomach.

"It's a lot to remember," she said in barely a whisper.

Staring into her eyes, he nodded. "I think that's it for today. How about a quick run to wind down?" Cool down was more like it. Her hot breath on his face and tiny hands on his shoulders was more than he could take. A run in the brisk air would be the perfect solution.

"I'll race you to the park." She pulled herself from his arms and shimmied under the ropes.

"You're on. I'll even give you a head start," he said, following her out of the ring.

Michelle laughed. "Head start? I was about to offer one to you. I was a distance runner in college."

"Well then, what are you waiting for, Willis?" Smiling, he headed for the door.

****

Going to the gym was a bad idea. No, it was a terrible one. She convinced herself she could distance her growing feeling for Hunter. She'd even learned how to wrap her hands so she didn't have to touch him. Correction: she taught herself so he wouldn't have a reason to touch her, because, damn it, his touch set off a million butterflies in her belly.

Their footfalls pounded the sidewalk in unison. Michelle concentrated on her breathing, taking deep breaths in through her nose and blowing out through her mouth. It was one of the first times she didn't have to worry about her surroundings and safety in public. She transferred that responsibility to Hunter. They ran in comfortable silence until they reached the park.

"You *are* a runner. You're not even out of breath." He laughed as he tried to catch his.

"It's all in the breathing. You have to practice regulating your breath. It's about taking long deep breaths of air into your lungs and letting it out slowly."

"The student teaches the master. How about we walk for a while? I want to show you one of my favorite spots in the city. It's just up that trail." He pointed to a narrow path cut through over grown bushes.

"Sure, I don't have to be at the gallery until eleven."

Hunter bought them each a bottle of water from a street cart and pointed toward a path.

Michelle scanned the park. She'd never actually stepped foot inside. It had always scared her to enter it alone. There were too many hidden areas. "It's so beautiful here."

"If you think this is beautiful, wait until you see what's around this bend."

Michelle smiled when she saw a small body of water come into view. She looked at Hunter and furrowed her brow. "The pond?"

"It's not just any pond. Go see what's inside," he said, nodding toward it.

Michelle moved closer to the edge and peered at the surface. A bright flash of color danced in the murky water. "What was that?"

"Fish. Look." He pointed at another flash of red and orange.

Michelle leaned over the water, bracing her hands above her knees. "Koi fish? How cool. I wonder how they got here."

Hunter squatted next to her. "Believe it or not, I put them here."

"You? Why?"

"It's a funny story. Someone brought two into the bar last year and asked me if they thought they'd survive if they let them go in the Hudson River."

Michelle laughed. "The river? Seriously?"

Hunter took a swig of water and chuckled. "Ridiculous, right? I took them and set them free here." He shrugged. "Figured they'd have a better chance in a pond than the river. I've been feeding them ever since, and I bring a new one every now and then to keep them happy." Hunter pulled a piece of bread wrapped in plastic out of his pocket. Tearing the bread apart, he gave half to Michelle. The fish quickly gobbled each piece as it floated on the water's surface.

"They certainly seem happy," Michelle said as she threw the rest of her bread into the pond. "It's a beautiful spot. Bet you take all the girls up here."

"Nope. You're the first."

"Uh-huh. And I have a bridge to sell you." She smirked.

"I'm serious. It's a place to be alone and think. Between the bar and Alex's apartment, I don't have much alone time."

Her gaze rested on his inked wrist. She reached for his hand and laced her fingers with his before pushing his sleeve up and exposing the design. "Your fish." She traced the lines of his tattoo and pointed to the pond. "Represents your fish."

He grinned and nodded. "Sounds silly, but I like to think I helped these little guys in some way." He shrugged and stuck his thumb over his shoulder. "Race you back?"

Their eyes locked for a moment. "You're on." She playfully pushed him and took off running.

The run blew new life into Michelle. There was no need to hide in the shadows or blend with the crowds.

Shoulders back and head high, she ran with confidence, her muscles awakening with each step. She slowed and peeked behind her shoulder, allowing him to catch up. "Hey, slow poke. I'm leaving you in the dust. Move your ass."

Hunter appeared at her side. "Maybe I like the view back there," he said through heavy breaths.

Michelle laughed and stopped at the corner as the light turned red. She narrowed her eyes and took a swig of water. "What? Why do you have a goofy grin on your face?" she asked after swallowing.

"Sorry. It's just you seem so happy. You normally look as though you have the weight of the world on your shoulders. Here. Now. You seem so… happy."

Calmness settled over her body. "I guess I never realized how much I missed running. It's been a long time."

"Why don't you run anymore?"

She rolled her eyes. "You don't want to know. It'll confirm my crazy status."

"Well, if you're crazy, I'm certifiable. Come on, we're friends, right? Tell me."

"I don't like to be vulnerable, and I can't run on the streets without having to watch my back. I feel safe with you. No one is going to mess with me while I'm being escorted by a musclehead."

"New York's not that dangerous. There's no reason why you can't take a run each morning. I'm sure Chinatown is hopping at an early hour. It's not like you live in some deserted area," he said.

"I know that, and you know that, but it still doesn't help my issue. It's something I have to work through." She looked down and suddenly the walls built up around her once more.

Hunter hooked his index finger under her chin. "Hey. Let me help you."

She shook her head. "That's nice of you. I tried a lot of things. It's just something I have to deal with. You may be able to help your fish, but I'm a lost cause." She glanced at her watch. "I gotta get ready for work. I'll take pity on you and walk back."

"You're too kind." He laughed, slipping his arm over her shoulder, and pulled her close. "Just so you know, I'm here for you. You're not alone."

Her hand slid around his back and hooked around his waist, closing the distance between them. Friend or otherwise, she couldn't stop the fire burning deep within her belly.

Chapter Eleven

A week of daily workouts left Michelle with a hunger for more. Her punches became harder, her stance tighter, her focus stronger. Even though she'd never felt better physically, the aggression she put into each workout continued in her dreams. Her nightmares were back with a vengeance. Most nights she'd sleep a handful of hours before waking with a gasp, tangled in sheets and covered in sweat. Details from the night of the attack prickled her skin. She'd tried so hard to lock those memories away, but the evil ugliness of that night rolled back into focus. Unlike the last time nightmares plagued her, she refused to take drugs to sweep them away. This time she'd deal with the memories. This time she was strong enough.

She pushed the gym door open. Oddly, she took comfort in the scent of sweat and dust wafting to her nostrils as she stepped inside.

"Hey, princess," Max called from the desk.

"Morning, Maxie." Michelle waved at the woman as she scanned the room. Her gaze landed on Hunter, already hard at work at the punching bag in their now-regular spot. His stiff stance and razor-sharp focus on the punching bag clued her into his less than happy mood. "Starting without me?" she asked, dropping her water bottle on the mat.

"Yeah. I had too much energy this morning, so I came in early," he said without stopping.

"Anything wrong?" Michelle asked, slipping her hands into her wraps.

Hunter threw a rapid succession of upper cuts before walking to the water fountain and taking a long sip. He turned and stared at her for a moment. "Do you ever feel like your life is going nowhere? Like you don't know what the hell you're doing?"

She straightened her back, surprised by the clipped tone of his voice. "Want to talk about something?"

Taking a deep breath, his eyes softened and a smile peeked through his lips. "I'm sorry. Alex pissed me off this morning. I won't bore you with details about the bar."

Michelle raised her arms and stretched, then bent each elbow and pressed in with the other hand to warm up her bicep muscles. "Maybe it's time to do something else with your life. Don't you have dreams and plans?"

He opened his mouth like he had something to say but shook his head slightly, bottling it back up in the dark hole of his thoughts. "Yeah, I have plans. Plans to give you a killer workout today. Are you ready for it?" And just like that, the Hunter she knew was back.

"I thought you were going to go easy on me today. I have pains where I never knew I even had any muscle." She exaggerated a wince.

"That means it's working. No pain, no gain, baby. Anyway, if you feel that way, I guess you don't want to try a jump kick today."

Her eyes opened wide, and suddenly her aches and pains didn't seem so bad. She'd asked him about jump kicks at the beginning of the week, but he'd said she wasn't ready yet. "A jump kick? Really? You're going to show me how?"

"Yeah, as long as you promise not to break anything. Let's get you warmed up first." Hunter took her though some cardio exercises and light punching before he moved her to an empty spot. "We can't have you falling on one of these old guys. They may like it too much." Hunter stuck his thumb behind him at one of the regulars.

"Hey! Who you calling old? I can kick your ass in the ring any day, young man," a gruff voice called.

Michelle peered around Hunter to the gray-haired man a few feet from them. "I think that was a challenge."

Hunter looked over his shoulder. "He probably can kick my ass," he said to Michelle before turning around. "You're right, Mr. Jensen. But right now, I'm going to show this young lady a jump front kick, and if she passes the test, I may even show her a jump roundhouse."

The man nodded. "Carry on, boy. I'll kick your ass later."

"That's kind of you, Mr. Jenson." They both laughed before Hunter took on a serious pose. "Ready to get started, grasshopper?"

"Lead the way, Master McAvery."

"Master, huh? I kind of like the sound of that," he said, raising a brow.

Michelle rolled her eyes. "Why does that not surprise me?"

"Okay, let's get serious. People have hurt themselves with these moves, so concentration on balance is important because you're taking off on one foot and landing on another. Watch." Hunter took a couple of steps back and jumped from his left to his right foot and kicked. The thump of the bag echoed through the gym. He held out his hand. "Try it."

Michelle stepped back and mimicked his movements, but shuffled her feet so she didn't get much air in her kick. A light thump hit the bag, barely moving it forward.

"Okay. Try it again."

She continued the movement until she stepped confidently, lifting her feet higher each time. In return the noise grew louder, and the bag even moved an inch or so.

"Good. You're getting the hang of it. Want to try the roundhouse now? It's a little trickier because while the front kick is a forward motion, the roundhouse is to the side. Since you're swiveling your body, there's more of a chance to twist your ankle or fall." He stepped back and performed a few on the bag. His high kicks were impressive.

"Man, with a kick like that, you can audition for the Rockettes."

A snort came from the side, and they turned to see Mr. Jensen laughing to himself. "She's a funny one." He pointed at Michelle.

"Nice. All right, smartass. Want to try it yourself?"

Michelle took her place in front of him. "I'm sure I won't get my kick as high as yours, but I'll give it a try."

She turned but second-guessed her footing, and her ankle gave out on her, sending her to the mat. Hunter was a step behind her and tried to break her fall, but they both ended up toppling to the floor. The now-familiar scent of Hunter surrounded Michelle as he held her in his arms. She was half on his lap. The fact that he didn't mind her body on him became evident on the back of her thigh. "I'm such a klutz. Sorry to fall on you."

His fingers stroked her arms for a moment. "Are you okay?" His husky voice seeped into her head, clouding her thoughts.

"Yeah. I'm fine. Maybe I should stick with front kicks next time." She giggled and bent forward, planting her hands on the mat to get off his lap as gracefully as possible.

"I think that's a plan. You coming back tomorrow?"

"You bet," Michelle said as Hunter stood.

"Why don't you just ask her to dinner already? Sheesh." Mr. Jensen furrowed his brow and swatted his hand. "Kids today," he mumbled and walked away.

Heat rose in her cheeks and she knew she must've turned a deep shade of red. "On that note, I'm out of here."

Hunter chuckled. "See you at the bar later?"

She shook her head. "Not coming in today. There's a new exhibit coming in and I have to help Cheyenne at the gallery." She'd spent more time at McAvery's than expected. It was time to pull her weight. "See you tomorrow." She hesitated. The answer to his earlier question sat heavy on her tongue. Yes, she often felt her life was going nowhere and questioned her decisions. But instead opening up to Hunter, she followed his lead and shoved her insecurities away. With a small wave, she left.

****

Hunter's gaze followed her out the door. He felt another set of eyes on him, and he glanced at the desk to meet Max's knowing grin. "What are you looking at, Maxie?" he called and then resumed his extended workout.

After another couple rounds on the speed bag, he finally felt human enough to go on with his day without ringing his brother's neck. Alex pulled rank on him that morning and ordered him to work an extra shift that day. He'd planned to begin studying for the certification exams he needed to go back to work in the finance industry. Alex's attitude confirmed his need to move on sooner than later. Hunter headed for the shower when Max blocked his path.

"You're doing a good job with her. You're good at helping people, Hunt. Why not let someone help you?"

"I'm doing fine." He wiped his brow and stepped around Max.

"You're forgetting who you're talking to. I was there from the beginning."

He stopped and took a deep breath before turning around. "I know. Sorry for being a prick. It's been a tough day."

She nodded but narrowed her eyes. "A tough day, huh? You infuriate me sometimes, do you know that? You have everything going for you. You're a young, good-looking, highly intelligent man who is pissing his life away in his brother's bar. Thank God you stopped drinking and screwing everything in sight, or I'd really need to hurt you. That's the only reason I haven't said anything to you lately. But you're becoming too comfortable, Hunter. I know you've had your share of tragedy, but it's time to move on. One year becomes two, two becomes five, and all of a sudden you've been on this plateau of a life for ten years and don't progress. I don't want that for you, and neither did your mother."

"Fuck, Maxie. Don't do this to me today." He wiped the sweat off his forehead with the back of his hand.

"If not now, then when?"

Hunter blew out a breath. "You sound like one of those posters on the wall."

"I promised your mother I'd look out for you. She always worried about you. She said you had more potential than your bigshot brothers, but you wouldn't let anyone see it, so you always let them take the spotlight."

Hunter nodded. Alex and Liam always competed with each other to be the fastest, strongest, and smartest. Hunter sat back and allowed them to fight over the number one spot. It wasn't until his brothers left for college that he gained confidence and found something he was good at. Upon his mother's insistence, he took up boxing in high school. Boxing not only made him more confident, the workouts also added muscles to his thin frame.

By the time his brothers returned home for the summer of their sophomore year of college, Hunter had towered over them and benched two hundred pounds. The twins had finally accepted Hunter as a peer instead of their baby brother. Things changed for the better between the McAvery brothers. However, their bond stretched to the limit when their mother was diagnosed with cancer that had already invaded most of her body's organs. It was the beginning of the end of everything Hunter knew and cherished.

"You think you have problems, but you're not the only one to have bad things happen. Old Mr. Jensen is dying. He has the same thing your mother did. Bet you didn't know that. Yet, he comes in here full of fight and energy. Just like she was until the end. The only time I see you like that is when you're angry. You need to channel that drive into something positive, because negativity will bring you down. And it's hard to come back after wallowing so long. Tell me, what's the deal with that girl?" Max nodded her head toward the entrance.

"Michelle? Nothing. She's doing some work in the bar, and I offered to show her some self-defense. That's all." Hunter shrugged.

"You're full of shit. She's different. You hardly ever bring anyone in here. I think the last time you did, you were both drunk off your asses. You brought Miss Barbie Doll through the door, and she squealed about the stench of the place, held her nose and left."

Hunter chuckled. "Oh yeah. I remember that. She wanted to know where my big muscles came from." Hunter raised his fist, showing Max his bicep.

She swatted him with the towel draped over her shoulder. "Put that thing away and listen to me. You need to move on. This girl, Michelle, she makes you happy, I can see it. Stop being such a pig-headed jerk and see what's right in front of you, not what happened in the past."

"I hear you, Max. But it's not as easy as you make it sound."

"Nothing worth having is easy to achieve. You have to fight for it," she said and punched him in his arm.

"Ouch. Damn, you missed your calling. You would've made a great inspirational speaker."

Mr. Jensen walked out of the locker room and Hunter gazed at his labored gait. "Thanks, Maxie! I'll see you bright and early tomorrow. Maybe I'll stop and pick you up one of those pastries you like so much."

"Sounds good. Looking forward to it, Stanley," Max called as she waved at the old man. She turned to Hunter and raised her eyebrows.

He nodded. "I get it, and you're right, as usual."

"Now, get your sweaty ass into the shower. You're stinking up the joint," she said, straightening her five-foot frame and giving him a push toward the locker room.

Hunter kissed Max on the cheek before heading for the door.

"What was that for?" she called to him.

Hunter held the door open and looked over his shoulder. "For kicking my butt when I need it, and for jogging my memory about what really matters in life."

Max nodded. "It's what I promised your mother, you know."

"I appreciate you looking out for me, even if you are a pain in the ass." Hunter shot her a smile before ducking into the locker room.

COLORS OF US

Chapter Twelve

Max's words unearthed feelings he'd shoved into the far corners of his mind. Hunter paced the bar like a caged animal all morning until Alex sent him out to run errands. He jumped at the chance to get away from the bar for a while and work off some of his nervous energy. McAvery's had been his salvation after the accident, but lately, it felt like a prison. It was time to finally move on and away from the city. Too many memories taunted him at every turn. A gust of early autumn wind blew against his face. A fresh start would do him well.

Hunter returned from the bank and corner produce market. Placing the bag of lemons and limes on the bar, he signaled to Mikey. "Put those in the fridge, would you?" he asked.

"Yeah. Hold on, you got a phone message from—" Mikey held up the scrap of paper and squinted. "Max. But she sounded like a chick with a cigar."

"Maxie?" Hunter furrowed his eyes and grabbed the message. "Did she say why she called?" She never called him. His skin prickled at the back of his neck.

"Nah, but she left her number. Said to call her right away."

Hunter leaned over the bar, picked up the receiver, and dialed the number Mikey had written on the scrap of paper. One ring after another sounded in his ear as dread dug a hole in his stomach. Finally she answered.

"It's Hunter."

"Where've you been? I tried your cell."

"Left it home. What's going on?"

"It's your friend Michelle. She came back this afternoon. Been here for a while, and there's something not right with her. You need to get down here."

"I'll be right there." Hunter hung up. "Watch the bar. I gotta run out. Tell Alex I'll be back soon," Hunter barked at Mikey as he raced out the door, picking up his pace from a fast walk to a jog.

Pushing open the door, his eyes fell on Max behind the desk. "What's up? Where's Michelle?" He followed Max's gaze to the corner of the gym. Michelle's hair was dark with sweat and stuck to her cheeks and neck. She pummeled the heavy bag with a succession of hard punches. The wires of white ear buds dangled from her ears, reminding him of the way she zoned out when she painted. "What's the matter? She looks like she's just focused on a hard workout."

Max shook her head. "It's more than that. I stepped behind the bag to check if she was okay. She just looked right through me. She's in a zone, but a dark one. I've seen that look before. Something's going on. What do you know about her?"

"I know she's afraid of everything. Her fear rules her life. She won't take a bus or the subway. Won't even leave her apartment when it's dark. I told you I brought her here to teach her self-defense. I'd hoped it would help."

"Hunter, look at her. She's punching that bag so hard her knuckles are bleeding. Go to her. Help her."

As he drew closer, deep bass beats filled the air around her. He didn't know Yo-Yo Ma's music, but he'd bet a round of drinks at the bar she wasn't listening to it. It sounded like some type of hard garage rock. She seemed unaware of his presence. His gaze washed over her reddened face as sweat dripped over her empty eyes.

"Fuck him. I should've fought. I should've fought back," she muttered through labored breath.

Hunter stepped behind the bag and waved his hand in front of her eyes. No reaction. "Michelle." He pulled the earbud wires from her ears.

Stopping for a moment, she curled her fingers into tight fists and continued with an onslaught of punches as though her life depended on her fight.

"Michelle. That's enough, sweetheart. Stop." He grabbed her wrists.

"No! I should've. I should've fought. Back. My fault. It was all my fault." Her chest rose and fell as sobs wracked her body.

"Shh. Shh. Breathe, it's okay."

Closing her eyes, she continued to fight him.

He let go of his grasp and accepted her punches to his chest and arms. Cupping her face with his palm, he brushed the hair from her eyes with his other hand. "Open your eyes, honey. You can do it."

Open your eyes, honey. You can do it. Visions of the night he said those exact words flashed into his head. He stared at the blood from her knuckles and saw Isabel's blood rushing from her head and soaking the T-shirt he used to try to stop it. *No. Not now.* He began to shake. Dropping to his knees, he took Michelle to the floor with him. He wrapped his arms around her and rocked her on his lap. "You'll be okay. You have to be okay."

You'll be okay. You have to be okay. Isabel's broken body flashed through his mind. Her limbs were tangled like a rag doll. He refused to look and kept his eyes focused on her face. Gathering her onto his lap, he rocked her broken body. *Open your eyes, honey. You can do it.*

Her eyelashes flutter and her gaze met his. "Hunter?"

"Don't worry, I have you." He brushed away the sweat-soaked strands of hair covering her eyes. Her smile

139

melted his heart. Without thinking, he bent his head and lightly brushed his lips over hers. The salty taste of sweat mixed with tears exploded on his lips. He needed more. Cradling her head in the crook of his arm, he pulled her close and coaxed her mouth open with his tongue.

Her hands snaked around his neck and her fingertips raked through his hair. She parted her lips, accepting his tongue as a soft moan filled his mouth.

He pulled away, cupped her chin in his palm and swiped the pad of his thumb over her bottom lip. "I'm sorry. I shouldn't have done that," he whispered.

"It's okay. I wanted you to." She smiled.

He studied her face for a moment and helped her to stand. "Let's sit on the bench over there, and I'll find some first aid supplies and cold water." Sliding his arm around her waist, he helped her sit before grabbing the first aid box and a couple of water bottles from Max at the front desk. "She's okay," he said unconvincingly.

Max's gaze traveled from him to Michelle. "You sure?"

"She has to be," he said quietly and returned to Michelle, approaching as she examined her hands.

"I can't believe I did this to myself." She wiggled her fingers. Three knuckles on both hands were oozing with blood.

"Let's take these off first." He slowly unwound the hand wraps and inspected the damaged knuckles. "You really did a job on your hands. Want to tell me what happened?"

"I don't know." She averted her eyes.

He gave her hands a small squeeze and her gaze returned to meet his. "You were talking about fighting back. Was it about the attack?"

Michelle looked down and nodded.

"What the hell happened to you?"

She shook her head.

His hands slid over her shoulders. "Hey, you can tell me. Please."

Michelle's gaze slowly met his. Wet lashes formed triangles as she blinked away tears. She took a deep breath. "Two years ago, I stayed on campus after my senior year to take a class I missed and needed for graduation. Everyone had moved out, but they let me stay to finish my class. This guy, a football player, had the same deal. We went out a few times before, but his drinking was out of control, and I told him I didn't want to see him anymore. One of the last nights there, he saw me at a club and tried to dance with me. He was all over me and reeked of alcohol. I told him to leave me alone, and I left. He showed up at my room that night. I don't even know how he got into the building." Michelle hissed as he dabbed the broken skin.

"Sorry, go on."

"He came to my door, acting all sweet. I opened the door just a crack, and he forced his way in." She sucked in a breath as though she were fighting for her last. "I told him to leave, but he kept saying I wanted him, I wanted it. I told him no. I. Said. No. But he didn't listen." She turned her face, and tears streamed down her cheeks, landing on his hands as he cleaned her wounds. "A security guard making his rounds heard the door hit the wall when he forced himself in. He pulled the guy off me before he could do anything."

Hunter stopped what he was doing and swore under his breath. "Fucker. Was he punished for what he did?"

"He did some jail time for assault. I had to go to court and face him. Know what he said to the judge?" Michelle's shoulders slumped, and she averted her eyes to the ground. "He said I wanted it, otherwise I would've fought harder."

"Jesus."

"Yeah. Nice, right? The sad part about it is I *believed* it for a long time. I mean, why didn't I fight back harder?" She shook her head and a lock of hair fell into her eyes. He tucked it behind her ear with his fingers and cupped her cheek, regaining her gaze.

A weak laugh escaped from her mouth. "I told you I was a fucked-up mess. But here's the thing. I spent the last couple of years hiding and avoiding because I didn't think I could protect myself. But something clicked today. An energy coursed through me, and I couldn't stop it. It just came pouring out." She pointed to the heavy bag. "I felt strong. For the first time, I have a little bit of my old self back." She wiped her eyes on her sleeve. "I have you to thank for that."

Hunter carefully dabbed first aid cream onto the cleaned wounds and wrapped each one with a bandage. A battle raged inside him, twisting his stomach into a jagged ball. Who was he kidding—he could clean her wounds and apply a bandage, but he couldn't be what she needed. He'd disappoint her in the end. He couldn't save her, just like he couldn't save Isabel. "You have nothing to thank me for. You did it all. I only showed you how." He brushed her bandaged knuckles lightly with his thumbs. "These should heal in a few days. A week, tops. No boxing for you until then."

She held her hands in front of her face and wiggled her fingers. "I'm going to hit the little girls' room."

Hunter's gaze followed her as she disappeared into the women's locker room. Scrubbing his hand along his face, he gathered the first aid kit supplies and walked slowly to the front desk. Placing the kit on the desk, he avoided eye contact with Max, who knew him better than he knew himself. "Tell her I had to leave."

"Hunter. Wait," Max's stern voice called as he swung open the door and took a few deep breaths before breaking into a fast jog.

His head spun. Images of Isabel floated in and out of his mind's eye. She trusted him and he let her down. He'd do the same to Michelle. *Fuck.* Why didn't he die instead of Isabel? It was a question he asked himself often. Death would've been easier than the prison of guilt he lived in. He escaped sometimes, but it always lurked in the shadows.

****

Michelle splashed water on her face and patted it dry with the coarse paper towel. She stared at her reflection. Damn, she looked like shit, with red puffy eyes and a blotchy complexion from crying. She'd never told anyone the details about the attack. How did she let the words flow so easily with him? The kiss. It consumed her at the same time as it set her free. She touched her fingers to her lips. She'd never been kissed like that. It was raw and real and burned hot within her even now. Friends sure as hell didn't kiss like that.

She was falling hard for Hunter McAvery.

Taking a deep breath, she pushed open the door, expecting to see his face waiting to walk her home. Her heart dropped as she scanned the gym, hoping he was in the men's room. Gathering her hand wraps and jacket into her arms, she waited.

"You okay?" Max's voice sounded from behind and a hand squeezed her shoulder.

Michelle spun around, meeting the woman's gaze. "He left, didn't he?" The pity in Max's eyes confirmed the answer.

"Hunter's… complicated. Give him a little time."

Michelle shook her head. "Time? For what? To find a way to tell me I'm…I'm bat-shit crazy? I opened up to him, thinking he'd understand. I don't get him. First he kisses me, and then tells me he wants to be friends. Then he kisses me again and leaves." Michelle waved her hand toward the door.

"And they say we're the fickle sex," Max said with a smile.

Michelle offered a weak smile in return. "Thanks for the use of your gym, Max. It was nice of you to let me come in for free to try it out for a few weeks. I don't think I'll be back, though." Tears threatened to appear as Michelle slipped her jacket on and turned toward the door.

"Hold on."

Michelle looked over her shoulder.

"Don't give up on him. You're good for each other."

She blew a frustrated breath. "He doesn't give me much choice. He's the one who left." She threw her hands in the air. "Not that I can't say I blame him."

"You have your demons to fight. Well, guess what, girl? So does he."

Chapter Thirteen

Hunter wanted to hit something. He couldn't even do that because Maxie would read him the riot act the moment he set foot into the gym, and he'd deserve every word too. Michelle opened up to him, and he threw her trust back in her face. To make matters worse, he'd kissing her, again.

To top off his retched mood, people dressed in business suits entered the bar in packs. Apparently one of the firms in the area had their regional sales folks in for the week. To rub more salt into his wound, strawberry daiquiri was the drink of choice. *Great.* The blender ran nonstop for almost an hour, grinding his dim headache into a thundering throb at his temples.

Hunter didn't notice Michelle walk in, but he caught her setting up her paints next to the mural. The earbud wires snaked up to her ears, signaling she didn't want to be bothered. He waited for her to ask him to fill the water cup she used to dip her brushes into. He wouldn't be able to talk to her much due to the crowd, but he'd at least connect with her and offer an apology. However, she carried the cup around the corner to the bathroom, instead of sliding it on the bar as she normally did. Damn it, that small deviation in her routine was like a drop kick to his gut. She didn't need him.

He put Mikey on blender duty as he filled beer orders. His gaze washed over the mural. It was almost complete. Michelle used a fine brush to add details to various faces sitting at the outdoor tables in the painted scene. He admired her focus and determination.

Finally, the last of the lunch mob paid their bill and headed out the door. Alex strode across the room from the kitchen. "I think we sold every burger in the joint. That was one of the busiest lunches we've had in a while."

"Tell me about it," Mikey said. "I thought the blender was going to explode."

"Those blender drinks pay your salary. I'm right about keeping them on the menu, huh?" Alex asked.

"You're always right, bro." Hunter rubbed his forehead and pulled a bottle of ibuprofen from behind the register.

Alex crossed his arms and studied the mural. "Almost finished?"

Michelle seemed to just notice him. She cocked her head and pulled one of the wires out of her ear. "Sorry?"

Alex pointed at the wall. "The mural. It's almost done."

She followed his gaze. "Yup, I'll be finished painting today. Then it'll need a couple of clear coats to keep it protected." She stepped back and smiled. "So, what do you think?"

"It looks fantastic. You've really exceeded my expectations." Alex turned toward Hunter. "What d'ya think, Hunt? Should we throw a party for the completion of the mural?"

"Sure, whatever you want." He gulped three pills down with a glass of water.

Alex shifted his gaze from Hunter to Michelle. "Hey, what happened to your fingers?" He pointed to her bandaged knuckles.

She waved her hand. "It's nothing. Just got a little carried away during a boxing workout. My hands are meant to hold paintbrushes, not punch inanimate objects." She pointed to the mural. "I'm going to get back to work so you have a reason to throw that party." Her fingers found the dangling earbud and popped it back into place.

Hunter felt the weight of a knowing stare and caught his brother's eyes. Alex raised his eyebrows and jerked his head toward Michelle, who was busy mixing paint colors. Hunter shook his head. Brother-speak for "I don't want to talk about it."

Another group of businessmen walked through the door, saving Hunter from a verbal lashing. Glancing at the men sliding onto barstools, Hunter swore under his breath. He'd choose a brawl with Alex over serving Greg Kroger, self-proclaimed hotshot investment banker, and his band of yes-men. Greg frequented McAvery's for a liquid lunch about once a week. He took the gold star for asshole of the year. The cocky jerk was even more unbearable when he had an audience, especially for any unsuspecting female within earshot.

Hunter caught Greg's hungry gaze on Michelle as he ordered their first round of drinks.

"Looks like the painting is almost done. I'm gonna miss watching that ass wiggle around." He nodded at Michelle and slid off his barstool while his cronies snickered. "I think it's time to get some of that ass."

Hunter was one step ahead of him. Before Greg reached Michelle, two hundred ten pounds of Hunter McAvery blocked his path. "What the fuck are you doing, Greg?"

"What does it look like I'm doing? I'm about to ask your artist friend out." He looked over Hunter's shoulder and attempted to step around him.

"I don't think so," Hunter bit out, grabbing his arm.

"Let go of me, man."

"As long as she's working here, she's off-limits."

Greg opened his mouth to speak when Hunter caught Alex rushing toward them. "What's going on here?" His gaze moved from man to man.

"Your bartender here thinks he can tell me who I can and can't talk to. I just want to ask that lovely lady out for a cup of coffee and talk to her about her art." Greg and Hunter stood face-to-face in a stare down.

"All right. I don't know what's going on, but you both need to leave her alone to finish her work. Your drinks are on the house today," Alex said to Greg before turning to Hunter. "In my office, now. Mikey, watch the bar," he ordered as he headed toward his office.

Hunter followed him and closed the door.

"What the fuck is going on with Michelle and you?"

"Absolutely nothing."

"Bullshit. The tension is as thick as a one-pound burger out there. And her knuckles? I knew she was going to Max's with you. How'd you let her do that to herself?"

Hunter dug the heels of his palms into his eyes. "I wasn't there when it happened. Max called me to help her. She's working through something that happened to her in college." Hunter slumped into one of Alex's chairs. "She broke down and told me about an attack—it scared the shit out of her. Still does. But the boxing is helping."

Alex winced. "Was she—"

Hunter shook his head. "Campus police got there in time, but not before the scumbag screwed with her head."

"I can't imagine anyone wanting to hurt her."

The statement kicked him in the gut. It was exactly what Hunter did: he hurt and confused someone who trusted him. What a fucking ass.

Alex narrowed his eyes and stared at Hunter. "That doesn't explain why she's giving you the silent treatment today. What else happened?"

Hunter stood, the chair scraping along the wooden floor before he sauntered to the door. He didn't need Alex's shit.

"Hunter?"

He stopped and turned around. "I fucking kissed her, and then I left without an explanation. She's hurt and pissed and it's my fault. Okay?"

"Shit, I told you to leave her alone if you were just going to string her along like the others. She's not one of those women we meet out there," Alex said, waving his hand at the door. "She doesn't understand the game. She doesn't want to understand it. She's too—"

"Good?" *And sweet and genuine and so fucking sexy.*

Alex nodded. "Yes, good. And she's good for you if you'd get your shit together," he said quietly.

Hunter ran his fingers through his hair. "I can't do it, Alex. I can't be who she needs me to be. I don't deserve someone like her. Not when—"

"Damn it. When are you going to cut yourself a break? The accident wasn't your fault. You deserve happiness too. You've been moping around this place for two years. Two years. It's time to move on."

Hunter nodded, his eyes fixed on Alex's. "I know. I just don't know how," he said, opening the office door.

****

Michelle stepped back to study the mural. *Almost.* She had to finish it as soon as possible and leave McAvery's forever. She couldn't stand being so close to the man she trusted with her secrets and fears, only to be humiliated and left alone. She sighed and carried the cup filled with murky paint water to the bathroom. Dumping the contents into the sink, she rinsed the cup and pulled a few paper towels from the dispenser before heading back. She stepped into the hallway as she wiped the cup dry and ran into a wall of muscle. Her head shot up and met Hunter's razor sharp stare.

"I'm sorry I left the gym like that yesterday. I—" he said.

Michelle tried to step around him in the narrow hallway. She had to get away. His voice, his scent, his *everything* threw her into a black hole where nothing made sense except being wrapped in his arms. *Stay strong.* I don't want to hear your excuse. I get it. I'm a head case. Just put me in your 'not my problem' category, and let's go our separate ways, okay?"

"I can't do that," he said huskily.

"Help me understand something. I overheard your argument with that guy. Greg? If you don't want me, why do you care if someone else asks me out? Is this some kind of game you're playing?"

Strong hands grabbed her arm, guiding her around the corner and out of view from the bar. He backed her against the wall, caging her in with his hands. "No games. Don't you get it? I want you. I want you so bad it scares me." His breath blew heavy above her, sending shivers down her spine.

Her hands stayed off his body, but just barely. Heat radiated onto her palms like a sensual invitation. Her gaze shot to his. They stared at each other for a long moment. Tentatively, she snaked a hand around his waist and palmed the planes of his back while her other hand explored the corded muscles of his arm. Tilting her face upward, their breath mingled for a moment before his lips crashed upon hers. She whimpered into his mouth as her hips bucked against his leg. He leaned into her body, his hardness straining through his jeans and warming her belly. Her tongue tangled with his as she fisted his hair. Pulling at his T-shirt, her fingertips found a soft patch of hair from his belly button to the waistband of his jeans.

She broke their kiss and skimmed her lips up his stubbled jawbone to his ear. "What are you doing to me?"

He cupped her cheek and pushed her head back, pinning her to the wall. Her gaze followed the planes of his face as his other hand slipped up her shirt. Her breath caught as his touch woke her body. It was as though a fire erupted within her belly that had been dormant for far too long.

He tipped his forehead to hers, their eyes locked. "I don't deserve you," he bit out between clenched teeth. His hand, hot on her bare skin, stilled for a moment before slipping away. He stepped back and walked away, leaving her cold in the dark hallway.

Michelle stood bewildered in the alcove of the restaurant and touched her fingertips to her lips. She followed him out of the hallway. His long strides took him to the other side of the room, where he pulled open the door and disappeared behind it.

She leaned against the wall and closed her eyes.

****

Eerie silence surrounded Michelle as she stepped into McAvery's early the next morning. Thankfully Alex gave her a key when she started the mural, though it was the first time she'd used it. Her booted footsteps sounded on the worn wood-planked floor as she scanned the bar and stopped at the spot where Hunter normally stood. She shook her head, pulled the can of shellac from the bag she carried, and set it on the floor in front of the mural. She'd planned to apply a coat of varnish, leave a note for Alex, and walk out of McAvery's forever.

She took a moment to admire her work and take a few pictures with her smart phone. The mural was the most daunting thing she'd ever painted, but the end result was perfect. The setting featured a number of bar patrons; some talking, some dancing, some simply eating and drinking. She'd painted a man and woman sitting at a table in the back who resembled Hunter and her. The man wore a sexy smile as the woman cocked her head in a flirty pose. It was how she preferred to remember Hunter.

She checked the time and made quick work of applying the clear coat. It would need one more later that day, but she'd send Cheyenne to do the job. She couldn't face Hunter. Not after he walked away from her again. How stupid could she be?

She packed her supplies and pulled a cocktail napkin from the bar. Jotting a quick note of thanks, she left the key Alex had given her, as well as her business card where he could mail a check for the remainder of the fee. Her heart sank when the door opened. Closing her eyes, she prayed anyone but Hunter entered.

"You're here early," a deep, friendly voice called out.

She smiled. "I can say the same about you." She grew to like Alex over the past two weeks. "I just finished up and was about to leave this note to say thank you and good-bye." She handed him the napkin.

He stepped forward and took the note from her hand. "Good-bye? You're coming to the party tomorrow right?"

Taking a deep breath, Michelle shook her head. "I don't think it's a good idea."

"I won't take no for an answer. The party is in your honor, my dear."

"The party is for the mural and to celebrate the history of McAvery's, but since you've been so nice to me, I'll promise to stop by. Thanks for everything." Handing him the key, she stood on tiptoes and kissed him on the cheek. She glanced back at the mural one more time before heading for the door.

"What's the real reason you don't want to come?" Alex asked.

She turned and considered his question.

"Is it Hunter?"

Michelle bit her lip. It wasn't just Hunter. It was Alex too. The McAverys started to become too familiar and comfortable. She'd opened up to Hunter, and he shut her out. She wasn't about to do that again. Not now. Not ever.

Michelle shook her head. "Hunter helped me. I'm sure he told you about my little episode at the gym. I'm better now, but I can't see him again. It wouldn't be good for either of us."

"Maybe it's exactly what you both need. I've never seen him act this way about a woman since—" Alex seemed to want to say more. "Well, let's say it's been a long time."

She searched his face. "Why are you telling me this?"

He stared at her for a moment, concern showed through his dark eyes. He raked his fingers through his hair. "I know something about missed opportunities." Alex's gaze drifted to the door. "It's rare to find someone who gets you. Really gets you," he muttered. He shook his head and smiled at Michelle. "Never mind. I'm rambling. See you tomorrow, right?"

She nodded. "Yeah, okay. I'll stop in."

COLORS OF US

Chapter Fourteen

Michelle paced outside the bar. The beat of the dance music vibrated through her body. The door opened, sounds of shouts and laughter poured into the sidewalk. Alex went all out on the party and hired a live band. She peered through the window at the bar's patrons. There were enough people to tunnel her way into the bar, have an obligatory drink with Alex, and head out the door without anyone knowing she'd left.

Pushing the door, she stepped inside as the live music and the buzz of the crowd filled her ears. She purposely turned away from the bar where she assumed Hunter would be stationed. On a mission to find Alex, she scanned the room; avoiding one McAvery brother and hoping to quickly find the other. Craning her neck, she wasn't paying attention to those around her, and she stepped on a foot while bumping into something tall and hard.

"I'm sorry—" She turned to face the person she'd stepped on. Looking up, she gazed into familiar eyes. "Oh, I didn't expect you out here."

"Yeah. Alex hired a temporary bartender because he wanted me to enjoy myself." He took a sip of his drink.

"I've never seen you drink." She pointed to his glass.

"I don't. It's ginger ale."

"So are you?" Michelle asked, raising her eyebrows.

"Am I what?" His eyes flicked around the room.

"Having a good time?"

Hunter glanced around again and shifted from one foot to another.

"There you are!" A female voice called.

A tall blonde in a very short miniskirt sauntered up to Hunter and put her arm around him. "I thought you disappeared, silly." She poked at his chest with a manicured index finger as the clear liquid of the drink she held splashed against the side of the glass.

Michelle snorted. "I guess that answers my question. Excuse me."

"Wait a minute. You'rrrre the art girl," the woman slurred. "You painted that." She spun around and lost her footing falling into Hunter.

"Whoa, Sam. You have to take it easy on the booze."

"You two have fun." Michelle couldn't get away quick enough and ignored Hunter as he called her name.

Moving farther into the room, she found Alex standing in front of the ropes that protected the mural from curious fingers. She suggested he should keep people from touching the paint until it had time to set for a few days. A group of people hanging on Alex's every word surrounded him as he passed around the picture Michelle had used as a guide to paint the scene.

Alex's face lit up when he saw her. "There she is, making a late appearance. Come on over here, Michelle." He reached for her hand and pulled her into the center of the circle. Wrapping his arm around her shoulder, he gave her a small hug. "I thought you were going to stand us up."

"I gave you my word, but I can't stay very long."

"I'll make sure you get home safe," Alex said with a smile. "Why don't you tell everyone about the mural and your other work for sale at the gallery? Did you hear me folks, *for sale*. Which means you should go buy a Michelle Willis original before you can't afford her."

Heat crept up her cheeks from his not-so-subtle endorsement, but she wasn't stupid. He presented her with a great opportunity to gain a few fans and possibly sell some art. Surprisingly, she enjoyed talking about her work in front of an audience. A crowd formed as more people shuffled over to hear the story of the mural. She explained how she'd developed a story about each grouping of bar patrons sitting at the tables and along the bar in the painting.

"What about that one?" A woman pointed to the back table with the couple resembling Hunter and her, which she'd purposely skipped over.

She stared at the couple in the mural before turning to the woman. "What do you think their story is?"

"Me? Oh, well, let me see." She squinted at the painting and smiled. "They're looking at each other as though there's no one else in the room. They're happy just being together."

Michelle nodded. "That's what I was thinking too." Her gaze moved to a few feet from the woman and met Hunter's stare. "But that's why they're called stories. Anyway, if you're interested in my work, please take a business card. The Locke Gallery is a few blocks away, right on Mercer Street." A line of people formed to take her card, and some even asked her to pose for pictures in front of the mural. A man she'd recognized from the bar approached when the crowd thinned.

"Hey, Michelle. I'm Greg, and I have to admit, you were the reason I ate lunch at McAvery's just about everyday for the last few weeks. It was fun to watch the progress on the mural. You were so focused on your work, you probably didn't realize you were putting on a show for the bar."

Michelle laughed. "A show? It's not all that interesting, but I'm glad you enjoyed watching the mural come to life."

"I'd like to see the rest of your art. I have a lot of rich clients who'd love to back a new artist."

"There was a time I'd consider that, but I don't need a backer. I think I'll do okay on my own. However, if you have any clients with an appreciation of art and would like to take a look at my work, please send them to the gallery."

Michelle tried to make a quick getaway from Greg, but he followed her to the bar and insisted on getting her a drink. She didn't want to be rude to a friend of Alex's, so she accepted a club soda and planned her excuse for leaving the party.

****

Hunter's blood boiled when Greg winked at him as he followed Michelle to the bar. Hunter kept his eyes fixed on the mural. It was all he could do not to grab Greg and beat the shit out of him. Breathing deeply to steady his nerves, he studied the painting. He cursed the constant reminder of Michelle every time he turned around. But at the same time, he was glad it was there. It was like seeing an old friend. His eyes traveled to the couple in the corner, the ones he knew Michelle painted of the two of them. They looked so happy and at peace. He wasn't sure if either one of them was capable of that type happiness. They were two jaded people who were far too young to be so cynical about life. He wondered why she made them look so carefree. Maybe it was what she'd hoped for too.

"There you are!" A shrill voice called from over his shoulder.

Hunter closed his eyes and blew out a deep breath. He knew it was a bad idea for Alex to hire a bartender so he could mingle with the crowd. He couldn't shake Samantha, who took on the role of clingy drunk. He was sure Michelle couldn't stand him even more than before if that was possible. As if that wasn't shitty enough, Michelle was batting her eyelashes at Greg Kroger. *Fuck!* He had to do something. The first order of business was to get rid of Samantha, and then he'd be able to talk to Michelle in private.

He spun around and took the glass from Samantha's unsteady hand. Placing it on an empty table, he guided her to the coat closet.

"Where are we going?" she squealed.

"I'm taking you home. You've had enough fun for one night."

Samantha's eyes lit up. "Really? You're taking me home?"

Hunter rolled his eyes. "It's not what you think. Let's go find your coat."

After entering the closet, Samantha shut the door and dragged her nails along Hunter's back as she pulled him into an embrace.

He grabbed her arms and unhooked the hold she had on him. "This isn't going to happen. Let's just find your coat."

She pushed out her lower lip in an exaggerated pout and yanked her coat from a hanger before he guided her out the front door. Thankfully, it only took a few minutes to hail a taxi. He opened the door and helped her inside. "Give the cabbie your address."

She moved over and patted the seat next to her. "Arrrren't you coming with me? Don't leave me lonely." She giggled.

His gaze moved from her to the sleazy-looking cabbie. He couldn't in his right mind let her go alone in that condition. He took a deep breath and glanced at the bar. "Move over," he said, climbing into the cab.

"I knew you'd change your mind," she whispered into his ear and ran her fingertips along his shoulder.

Hunter pulled her hand away and placed it on her lap. "It's not gonna happen, Sam. I just want to make sure you get home safe."

"Okay," she said quietly. They rode in silence for a few minutes before she folded her arms and pouted. "So, what changed? We had some good times."

Hunter chuckled. "Yeah, I guess we did. I met someone who changed the way I look at things lately. She hates my fucking guts and I blew any chance I have with her, but like it or not, she changed me."

Samantha slid away from Hunter and faced the window. "So it's the old 'it's not you, it's me' brush off, huh?"

The cab came to a stop outside Samantha's building. Hunter asked the cabbie to wait while he helped her out and walked her to the door. "Sorry."

Samantha fished her keys from her purse. "You'rrrre a good guy. Save your apology for her. It's never too late to ssssay I'm sorry." She giggled loudly and stamped her foot. "Shit. I sound like a sappy greeting card, don't I?"

Hunter chuckled and held the door open as Samantha stepped inside. He closed it and checked it was locked before heading back to the waiting cab. "Back to McAvery's, and there's another twenty in it for you if you can get me there in five minutes."

Peeling a fifty from his wallet, Hunter passed the bill to the cabbie and opened the door before it came to a stop in front of the bar. Striding to the entrance, adrenaline coursed through his veins. He'd find Michelle and tell her everything. What the hell did he have to lose, anyway? As his fingers curled around the handle, a familiar laugh from behind him filled his ears. Dread sank to the bottom of his stomach when he glanced at the corner.

Michelle stood waiting for the light to change next to Greg "the asshole" Kruger. What. The Fuck. *You blew it again, McAvery.*

COLORS OF US

Chapter Fifteen

Crash.

A scream woke Hunter from a sound sleep. He sat up and scanned his bedroom for a weapon and reached for his old baseball bat in the corner.

"What a dick!"

Hunter breathed a sigh of relief. It wasn't a break-in, but Jacey's outburst warned Hunter he would spend the next hour cleaning up the aftermath of Alex's mess. He knew the drill, and he'd make his brother pay later.

He should've known something was up. Jacey was noticeably missing from the party the night before. Hunter figured she had been called into work at the last minute. Unfortunately, an explanation of her missing status arrived bright and early in the form of yells, sobs, and an occasional crash outside his bedroom door. He rubbed his face and pulled on a pair of sweatpants.

He found her sitting on the floor of the kitchen among pieces of broken ceramic dishes. She held a white envelope Hunter knew was stuffed with cash. "I'm so stupid. Why did I think I was any different from the others? He never cared about me." She looked up at him with red-rimmed eyes.

Damn Alex. Hunter knew the routine. Reaching down, he helped her stand. "Come on, let's get you over to the couch." He guided her around the broken pieces and grabbed a few napkins from the counter. "He cared about you, Jace. Alex is just incapable of having a longtime relationship." It was the truth, and the same line he used on all of Alex's conquests.

"Don't make excuses for him. He's a prick," Jacey choked out.

Hunter chuckled and squeezed her hand. "No argument there. I have something to take the sting out." He moved to the kitchen and took down a bottle of Jose Cuervo and a shot glass from the cabinet. He wasn't an advocate of tequila in the morning, but judging by her wrinkled clothes and smeared makeup, he suspected Jacey hadn't been to bed yet, so he made an exception.

After calming her down, he helped her pack the few things she had kept at their apartment, called her a cab, and walked her out. They stood in awkward silence on the sidewalk. "I'm sorry, Jace." It was the only thing left to say.

Jacey closed her eyes and shook her head. "I knew what I was getting into. It's fine. I think I've had enough of the McAverys for a while." Her gaze flicked to him. "No offense."

Hunter snorted. "None taken." Jacey wasn't the only person with that sentiment.

The cab pulled alongside the curb, and Jacey folded her long legs into the back seat.

"Take care," Hunter said, placing her box of hair products and makeup on the seat. Jacey gave him the benefit of a nod as he closed the door and watched the cab pull away. Hunter realized she was the second pissed-off woman he'd helped into a taxi within the past twenty-four hours.

****

Hunter stormed into his brother's office. "How about giving me some notice next time?"

Alex's eyes remained fixed on his laptop. "Notice? For what?"

"Don't act stupid. I woke to Jacey's rants and sobs as she packed her shit. Then out of default, I was her shoulder to cry on. You could've warned me it was coming so I could've made a quick getaway with you. I was like a sitting duck as dishes went flying."

Alex cringed. "That bad, huh?"

"Yeah, it was that bad. I took care of her, and she was in decent shape when I loaded her into a cab, but you have a big mess to clean up on the kitchen floor. And you'll need to buy more plates."

Alex took a deep breath. "Look, I'm sorry, man. Did she get the envelope I left on the kitchen counter?"

"Yeah, she got it. She said the parting gift was your calling card. Then she called you a prick. Can't say I don't agree with her."

Alex smiled. "I owe you one."

"You owe me more than one, bro. Your track record sucks. How many hearts are you gonna break before you settle down?" Hunter picked up the cocktail napkin with a phone number written in curly handwriting off Alex's desk. "Picked up another one last night at the party? Is this your next conquest? How much is this one worth?"

He swiped the napkin from Hunter's hand. "Don't judge, Hunt. You're not much better."

"At least I don't make any promises. Women know exactly where I stand and what I want."

"What about Michelle?" Alex raised his eyebrows.

"What about her?"

Alex stood and glared at Hunter. "You got in her head, man, and then you rejected her. What you did to her was worse than what just happened with Jacey. Michelle was vulnerable and broken, and you took advantage of that."

"I-I—" Hunter sank into a chair and rubbed his eyes. "Shit. I fucked up."

Alex blew out a breath and leaned on the edge of his desk. "We both did, but you can still fix your problems. Mine are too far gone."

"I don't know how, Alex. I want to, but I don't know how to stop feeling this way."

"Maybe you should go talk to someone again," Alex said quietly.

"Like it really helped me last time. They'll just load me up with prescriptions and send me on my way." He had enough of telling perfect strangers about his problems. Talking wasn't going to change the fact that he was responsible for someone's death. Someone who trusted him. Someone who loved him.

Hunter swallowed and looked up at Alex. "I think it's time for me to move on with my life. I need to get out of here."

Alex took a deep breath and let it out slowly. "I'd hate to see you go, but yeah. It's time, bro."

Hunter nodded and pulled his wallet out of his pocket. He set it on the desk and found the dog-eared business card he'd kept behind his driver's license for the past two years. Swiping the pad of his thumb over the corner, the muffled flip of the card stock perked his ears and increased the beat of his heart. Every once in a while, he'd taken the card out of its slot and stared at it, only to tuck it back into its place. It was time to use it and he hoped it wasn't too late. "May I?" Hunter pointed to the phone on Alex's desk.

"Take all of the time you need," Alex said and left the office.

****

Michelle wrapped her arms around her chest as she stepped outside, deciding it was too cold to ride her bike to the gallery. Running back upstairs to her studio, she grabbed the scarf Miranda had given her last year and started the ten-block walk to SoHo. Tucking her chin into the soft fabric, she closed her eyes as the wind blew through her hair. Her feet stayed warm thanks to the shearling boots she wore, also from Miranda. She missed her friend and hoped she was having fun at the tail end of her trip to Europe.

Glancing into the window of Primo Java as she walked by, Michelle did a double take at the head of curly black hair. Her line of sight followed to the woman's trim waist and long stockinged legs. The woman standing in line at Primo Java could've been Miranda Locke's twin. Michelle smiled and continued walking toward the gallery. She was excited Miranda was returning the following week and planned a small party for her return. The party planning kept Michelle from missing going to McAvery's everyday. Even though things ended on a sour note with Hunter, she still missed the excitement of working on the mural. She thought about advertising with a few of the local websites and newspapers. She'd love to work on another mural, and there were plenty of restaurants and bars in the area.

She unlocked the front door to the gallery and noticed the lights on in the back. Cheyenne was good about turning off the lights before closing, and it was unusual for them to be on when she opened the gallery. Stepping to the back, her footsteps echoed through the rooms. As she entered the office, she noticed a battered brown leather bag sitting on the desk. She'd know that bag anywhere. Her face lit up when the front door opened, and Michelle ran to the front of the gallery.

"Miranda?" She rushed the woman who held two cups of coffee.

"Hold on, little one. Let me put these down and give you a proper hug." Miranda strode to the front desk and set the coffees on the surface. Turning, she held out her arms.

Michelle practically knocked her down with a tight hug. "I can't believe you're back. We didn't expect you to return until next week." Michelle loosened her hold and pulled back. "Is everything okay?"

Miranda laughed and stroked her hair. "You worry so much. Everything's fine."

"Then why did you cut your trip short?" she asked while searching her eyes.

"I got done what I needed to do, and I just had the feeling I was needed back here." She turned and picked up the coffee cups. "Let's go to the back with these. I want to hear all about what's been going on in your life over the past few weeks."

Michelle took one of the cups from her and Miranda wrapped her hand around her shoulder. "It's good to have you back."

"It's good to be back. Here, sit." She pulled out a chair from the desk as they entered the office. "I hear the mural came out really well."

Michelle tilted her head. "It did. I'm pretty proud of it. Who told you?"

Miranda lifted her bag and set it on her lap. She dug through the pockets until she found her phone and swiped her finger over the screen. "See, I have pictures of it, and you."

Michelle took the phone from her friend's hand and examined the pictures. They were taken the night of the party. "Who sent these to you?"

"Alex." She leaned in close as Michelle's fingers advanced the pictures. "I love this one. You look so happy."

Michelle studied the picture and remembered that moment. It was one of the first times she felt comfortable talking in a crowd of strangers.

"I'm proud of you, little one."

"Lots of things have changed for me over the past few weeks."

Miranda searched Michelle's face. "So why do you look so sad?"

"Let me guess, Alex told you what was going on. At least what he thinks is going on, and you came home early because you were worried about me." Michelle folded her arms.

Miranda took a deep breath. "I won't lie to you. Alex is worried about you, and at the risk of feeling my wrath, he called to let me know you and Hunter were involved in some way. Is that true?"

Michelle stood and walked to the window. Staring at the shriveling garden of plants, she thought about the past few weeks with Hunter. "I wouldn't say we were involved. We became friends. We kissed, but that's it. He's moved on, just like the manwhore he is. I should've known. Cheyenne warned me about those two." Michelle turned toward Miranda. "Is it true you and Alex had a thing?"

Miranda nodded. "It was a long time ago, just before I bought the gallery. I was trying to get someone to display my art. Just like you, I walked my samples from gallery to gallery, presenting my work to owners and buyers. No one wanted to give me a chance. I stopped at McAvery's for a glass of water. I couldn't afford even a soda at that time in my life. The bartender was about to give me a hard time when Alex walked by and sat down next to me. We started talking, and he worked the McAvery magic on me. I fell for him hook, line, and sinker."

"The McAvery men seem to have that effect." Michelle pictured Hunter's dark eyes and crooked smile. She shook her head in an unsuccessful attempt to rid him of her thoughts. "How long were you with him?"

"Oh, probably a little less than a year. It was much longer than his usual tenure with women. It was a crazy time in our lives. His mother had just died and left him with the bar, and I was trying to make a living as an artist. He was the one who convinced me to open the gallery. He helped me find this spot and even assisted in negotiations with the sale. I hate to admit it and I'd never tell him this, but I owe much of my success to Alex McAvery."

"Why did it end?" Michelle hoped she wasn't prying.

Miranda tucked a stray curl behind her ear and it bounced back to the same position. "I found him in a compromising position with another woman at the bar. I walked out and told him I'd never step foot in McAvery's or look at his sorry-ass face again. And I never have." Miranda smiled. "I think that's why he sent me the pictures. He knew I wanted to see the mural, but my pride would keep me from going there."

"Wow. It's crazy that I ended up working there, huh?"

"I was shocked when I heard you were doing the mural for him, but I wouldn't talk you out of it. It was a great experience for you. I did, however, place a call to Alex and tell him you were off-limits to him and his little brother."

"Yeah. Back to Hunter. He's moved on, and it's time I do the same. So you did come back early for me, didn't you?"

Miranda smiled and nodded. "You've gone through so much hurt at such a young age. I didn't want you to suffer through a broken heart alone." Don't forget, I know how potent a McAvery can be."

A tear escaped and trickled down Michelle's cheek. She tried to stay composed, but having Miranda by her side meant she could breakdown, even if it was just for an afternoon. She wasn't alone in the world.

"Come here, little one." Miranda held her arms open, and Michelle moved to her and more tears fell.

"Damn it, I think I love him," she whispered through her sobs.

COLORS OF US

Chapter Sixteen

Hunter paced the floor outside Alex's office. He wasn't sure how to lay the landmine on Alex, but it had to be done. The knot in his stomach tightened as he turned the knob and pushed open the door.

Alex looked up. "Hey, just the guy I need to see. I'm about to place the Guinness order. How many kegs did we go through over the weekend?"

Hunter strode to the desk. "We have to talk, Al."

Alex swiveled his chair and faced Hunter. "What's up?"

Hunter took a deep breath. "I accepted a job in LA."

Alex paused a moment before speaking. "Los Angeles? Does this have anything to do with Liam?" Alex asked, hurt evident in his eyes.

Hunter nodded. "I need to move on with my life. Part of that is facing Lee and coming to terms with why he did what he did."

Alex slammed his fist on his desk. "Damn it, Hunter. He up and left us at a time when we needed him most. When *I* needed him most. He left me to take care of everything. You, the bar—everything! I don't understand why you're trying to kiss up to him now. You think he gives two shits about us? Why?"

"Why? Because I plan to beat the shit out of him until he gives me a good enough reason. If I don't get one, then at least I got to give him what he deserves. Anyway, he's not the only reason I'm going to LA. I landed a job out there. Call me an idiot, but I see it as a sign. I'm meant to go out there right now, and I'm going to face all of my ghosts. Liam is one of them."

Alex searched his eyes. "When you said you were ready to move on, I had no idea you were looking to leave New York."

"I wasn't planning to, but I contacted one of the VPs from my old firm. He gave me his card when I left and told me to call him if I ever wanted to return. Turns out he's working in the Los Angeles office and there was a job opening there. It's pretty much entry level, but it's a start, and most of all, it's the change I need."

After a couple weeks of phone and video interviews, Matthew James offered Hunter a job in the satellite office of Westinghouse and Todd as an associate asset manager. Hunter had climbed the ladder in the two years he worked for the firm before the accident, and he looked forward to jumping back into his career. A new sense of energy flowed through his veins at the thought of starting his life again.

"You're doing so well. I'd hate for anything to happen to cause you a… set back and I'm not there to help you."

"I'm not going to start drinking again, if that's what you're talking about." Hunter shook his head. "It's not going to happen. It's too big of a hole to climb out of. I'm out now. It's not a place I want to go back to."

Alex stood and approached Hunter. "You know I'm always here for you."

"Yeah, I know you are," Hunter said, slapping his brother on the back. He'd never forget the sacrifices Alex made for him.

"Be sure to give Lee an extra right hook to the nose for me, dude. If I go out there, I'd kill him."

"I know." Hunter searched his brother's eyes. His normal cool as a cucumber exterior was cracked and exposed. Liam was the only one to do that to him. One mention of his name put Alex in a dark mood for days.

Liam hurt both of them by abandoning them the day after their mother's death. Hunter was young and didn't understand the full extent of his brother's actions. Alex took the full brunt, and the fact that Liam was Alex's his twin doubled the punch. He left Alex to not only arrange the funeral, but he was forced to leave school and take over the bar. It was their only source of income and the reason Hunter was able to go to college. Alex could've cut Hunter loose. He was eighteen at the time, but upon Alex's insistence, Hunter followed through on his plans to continue his education. Alex sacrificed for Hunter, and Hunter would never forget it. He knew the news of him reaching out to his other brother was a blow to Alex. However, he also knew it was the right thing to do. Something told him it was.

"When do you leave?"

"Tomorrow."

Alex blew out a breath. "Doesn't give you much time. Do you have a place to stay?"

"There's a training program starting next week. They're putting me up in an apartment until I find a place to live."

Alex nodded. "I'm gonna miss you around here."

Hunter scanned the bar, his eyes resting on the mural. "I have to see Michelle before I go. Even if she won't talk to me, I have to tell her I'm sorry."

Alex cocked his eyebrow. "I hear Miranda is back in town. You better be careful—she'll eat you up and spit you out before you can escape. If you hurt Michelle as bad as I think you did, you'll be on her shit list for sure."

"I can handle it, bro."

"Yeah, that's what they all say. You haven't met Miranda."

****

Hunter strode into the gallery and recognized Cheyenne, Michelle's pink-haired coworker, from the first time he walked into Locke Gallery with Jacey. That was only a couple of months ago, but he felt as if much more time had passed. Glancing at Michelle's self-portraits still hanging next to the gallery window, Hunter closed his eyes to avoid the pain and sadness depicted in her expression.

"She's not here," Cheyenne called to him.

Hunter swung around to ask where he could find Michelle when the desk's phone buzzed.

Cheyenne held out her index finger and answered the phone. "Hi Miranda. Yes… yes. Um, yes." She whispered something into the phone. "Okay, I'll send him back." Placing the receiver on the phone cradle, she stared at Hunter. "Miranda Locke would like to see you. She's in the office, just walk straight back."

"Um, thanks," Hunter said uneasily. He strode to the back of the gallery until he saw a woman with sharp, assessing eyes. Her curly black hair spilled over her shoulders.

Approaching Hunter, she held her right hand out. "I'm Miranda Locke."

He shook her hand. "Hunter McAvery. I'm a friend of Michelle's."

Miranda cocked her head to the side and smiled. "I know."

"Do you know where she is? I really need to talk to her."

Miranda studied his face. "Damn, you look so much like Alex. Sit down for a moment, won't you?" She gestured to the door of what looked to be an office.

Hunter waited for Miranda to sit at her desk before pulling one of the empty chairs over and sitting.

His eyes traveled to a painting above her desk of two entwined bodies, one with pale skin, the other a warm shade of mocha. His gaze traveled to the woman with the exact shade of skin staring at him. He placed his elbows on his knees and leaned forward. "Is everything okay with Michelle?"

"Yes, yes. She's fine. That's not why I asked to talk to you. I've known Michelle for a year or so, and I have to say, she's changed. I think... no, I know, it has something to do with you."

Hunter smiled. "We got to know each other well while she painted the mural at the bar. I hope she didn't get in trouble for spending so much time there."

"Of course not. I've been after her to get out more. It was good for her. But she said you two decided not to see each other again. So, why are you here?" Even though her voice was calm, Hunter could tell she wasn't exactly pleased with him.

"To say good-bye. I'm leaving for California in the morning."

Miranda nodded slowly. "I see. Well, she went out. I'm not sure when she'll be back, but I'll tell her you stopped by." She stood, seemingly waiting for him to do the same.

Hunter stood to leave but sat back down on the chair and scrubbed his palm over his face before meeting the woman's stare. "I really need to see her, and I think you know where she is."

Miranda took a deep breath. "She went for a run. She takes the same path each day to the park to feed some fish in a pond, and then she heads home. She left about fifteen minutes ago, so she's probably at the park now."

Hunter sprang from the chair. "Thank you. I got to go."

"Hold on." A slim hand reached out and grabbed his wrist. "I know the way you McAverys work. Don't hurt her anymore than you already have."

The comment sliced through his gut. "I never meant to hurt her, Miranda."

"Go on." She waved her hand and turned to face her desk.

Hunter swiveled and ran through the gallery, his heavy boots clopping on the old wooden floor. Swinging open the door, he headed south on Canal to the same park they ran to a few weeks earlier. It was hard for him to run it in running shoes and doubly tough to get any type of speed with his boots. Huffing and puffing, he made it to the entrance of the park. Heading up the path, he scanned the faces walking toward him. As he crested the small hill, he spotted her long dark hair blowing in the wind as she threw pieces of bread into the water.

"Hey," he called.

Her back straightened and she turned slowly. "Hey yourself."

"You don't seem too surprised to see me."

She pulled her phone from her back pocket.

Hunter chuckled. "Of course. You were warned, huh?" He held out his hand. "May I?"

She ripped the slice of bread in half and handed him a piece.

"How are you?" he asked as he threw small chunks of bread into the water.

"Doing well. I got some business from the party. I've been consigned to paint a few portraits, and I used the generous bonus from Alex to get some MMA training at a gym in Chinatown. I feel stronger than I've felt in a long time."

Hunter crossed his arms. "That's good to hear, and how are things with Greg?"

Michelle narrowed her eyes. "Who?"

"You know, Investment Banker Greg. From the bar? You two left together the night of the party."

"Yeah, he insisted on walking me home that night. He said he promised Alex I'd get home safely. When he went in for a kiss goodnight, I kneed him in the nuts."

Hunter snorted. "You didn't."

"I did. And you know what, it was quite liberating." She laughed. "Speaking of the party, how's Samantha? She couldn't keep her hands off of you that night, and I saw you two leave together."

"There's nothing with Sam and me. There never was and never will be. I took her home so you and I could talk, but I was too late. You'd already left, with him."

Michelle took a deep breath and blew it out slowly before turning to face Hunter. "Why are you here?"

"I need to tell you something about me, about my feelings for you, before I leave."

"Leave?"

"I'm moving to California. New start, new job. But I couldn't leave without explaining why I acted like such an ass with you."

"I'm listening."

Hunter scanned the small pond as he carefully chose his words. His gaze landed on two red flowers. "Did you plant those?"

She chuckled. "They're not real, but it adds beauty to the dreary winter scene. Don't you think? I hate when everything is gray and bleak."

He turned to face her and studied her eyes and her soft features. "That's how you make me feel. You're the flower growing in my hell."

"What are you talking about?"

He cleared his throat. "I was engaged a few years ago. Her name was Isabel. We met in college. After graduation, she moved to New York with me so I could look for a job. Alex let us stay with him until we were on our feet. I landed a job at a Wall Street firm. It came with a huge salary and bonus. Everything was looking up. I bought Izzy an engagement ring and something else I always wanted: a motorcycle." Hunter took a deep breath. "She loved riding on the back of that thing. Said it made her feel free and alive. One day we were riding around the city. It was just a joyride. I rounded a turn and accelerated, and a guy in a parked car swung open the door. I swerved and hit my breaks to avoid hitting him. Isabel was thrown from the motorcycle, and her helmet came loose. Her head hit the pavement hard. There was blood everywhere. She died in my arms." He turned to Michelle. The look in her eyes wasn't one of pity as he'd seen from countless others throughout the years. Instead, understanding reflected in her eyes.

He swallowed hard. "After that, I wanted to die. I was supposed to be the dead one, not her. It was my fault. I blew my life up in that one wrong turn. She died because of me. I couldn't function after the accident. I resigned from my job and sat on Alex's couch for months before he enrolled me in bartender school and gave me a job so I'd have a reason to wake up in the morning. I've gone through the past two years like a zombie. I've jumped from one meaningless relationship to the next. Trying to forget. Trying to make the hurt go away. Until I met you. You awoke something in me. I felt things for you I never even felt with Isabel, and that scared me. But as much as I wanted you, I didn't deserve you. I don't deserve to be happy, not when I was the cause of someone losing their life."

Michelle walked to him and slipped her arms around his waist. "It doesn't sound to me that you were the cause. Sounds like it was an accident. A devastatingly tragic fluke of an accident." She stared into his soul through a veil of eyelashes. "Everyone deserves to be happy."

"I'm starting to accept that. It's the reason I need a fresh start in another place. There are too many memories here. If I'm going to move on, I need to make this change."

She nodded. "I'll miss you."

He gathered her into his arms and squeezed. Warmth radiated from her body, he felt her heartbeat matching his own. She was so alive. "Will you be okay?" he whispered into her hair. He loved how her hair smelled like a tropical breeze.

Michelle nodded into his chest. "I think so. Yes." She pulled away from his embrace. "I have something to show you." She slipped the backpack from her shoulder and pulled out a small notebook. "It's a poem I wrote. It's called Before You."

"Read it to me," he said huskily.

She turned a few pages of the paper and glanced at him before starting to read.

"Before you,
I walked through life without making a sound
I hid in shadows, I cried in silence.
Before you,
I simply survived.
Like a window, you opened my soul.
You brought me courage and hope
You helped me stand proud and strong.
You gave me a reason to live."
She closed the notebook as her face flushed.
"It's beautiful."

Michelle cocked her head, and her glossy dark hair spilled over her shoulders. "It's about you."

He touched her face and tucked a lock of hair behind her ear. "You know, we never had the chance to go on a date. How about having dinner with me tonight? Right now."

"Now?" Michelle looked down at her running clothes. "I can't go out like this."

"Come on. We'll swing by your apartment so you can change."

****

Hunter slipped his hand into hers as they left the park and headed toward her apartment. A gust of wind blew through her hair.

She turned to Hunter. "You're going to miss New York, you know."

"I'm going to miss certain things." He smiled and brushed his thumb along her hand as they walked side by side.

"Why California? Can't get far enough away?"

"I have to get out of New York. There are too many memories. I got in touch with the investment firm I worked for before the accident, and they offered me a job in their LA office. Plus, my other brother lives in LA."

"Alex's twin."

"Yup. He hasn't been around since our mother died, and I'm not exactly sure why. Alex won't talk about it and Liam hasn't reached out or returned my calls. It's time to get things out in the open. It may help all of us move on. Even Alex."

She glanced at him from the corner of her eye. There was a spark in him she'd only seen fleeting glimpses of in the past. "I'm really happy for you. You're piecing your life back together."

"I've got a long way to go, and I'm scared as hell, but it feels right."

Michelle sucked in a breath and covered her mouth in mock surprise. "Did the big, bad Hunter McAvery say he was... scared?"

He pulled her hand from her face and laced his fingers between hers. "Smartass."

They walked in silence of the remaining blocks to her apartment. He didn't loosen his grasp on her hand, and she had no plans of pulling away. Every once in a while, his thumb skimmed over the inside of her palm, putting her body on high alert.

She swallowed hard as they climbed the steps to her building. The right thing to do was to leave him on the steps while she changed her clothes. That'd be the responsible thing to do. That'd be the safe thing to do. But Michelle wasn't feeling responsible or safe. Each step they took toward the privacy of her apartment, each squeeze of his fingers, every sideways glance told her they both knew where they were headed.

COLORS OF US

Chapter Seventeen

What are you doing, McAvery? An internal badguy/goodguy war battled in his head, and the bad guy was winning by a long shot. He watched as she slowly flipped through her keys, buying time, probably having the same debate with her own alter ego. He stepped into the recessed entryway, ghosting against her back. He was about to make the decision easy for her.

Grabbing her wrist, he turned her around and pinned her to the door, her keys dropping with a clang on the floor. His hand trailed up her side, cupping her breast, before his fingers rested on her neck. Her pulse drummed against the pads of his fingertips.

She tipped her chin up to meet his gaze, her breath heavy on his lips.

"I want you more than I have anyone or anything in my life. I can't promise you anything past this minute. So say the word, and I'll walk away. But if you let me in, I promise to love you like you deserve. I plan to explore every inch of your body, to learn what makes you sigh and moan." His voice hitched in her ear.

Michelle's breath blew ragged, intermingling with his. "I shouldn't. We shouldn't." Her fingers raked through his tangled hair at the base of his neck, pulling at a few loose knots. She forced his head down while lifting her lips to his.

"Fuck." His mouth crashed down on hers as he cupped her face in his hands.

Her fingers snaked up his shirt and scratched his chest. "Take me inside, Hunter," she whispered into his mouth.

He broke their kiss and swooped down to pick up her key ring. She took it from him with shaky fingers.

Grabbing her hand before she could insert the key into the lock, he gazed down at her with a silent question. Her sapphire eyes burned deep into his soul. She nodded slowly and turned the key.

They entered the studio apartment lit only by the setting sun and city lights. Hunter lifted her easily into his arms and carried her to her full-size bed in the corner of her small room while she shrugged off her jacket and dropped it on the floor. He gently set her on the edge of her bed. She reached for the bottom of her T-shirt, but he stopped her.

"Let me." He knelt on the floor in front of her and pulled her shirt over her head before unhooking the back closure of her bra, allowing her breasts free. He'd dreamed about her pert breasts and took a moment to admire her beauty. Her dusky rose-tipped nipples hardened at his touch as he rubbed the pad of his thumb over their peaks, eliciting a small moan. "See, I've already learned one of your secrets."

She reached around his shoulders, pulled his shirt off, and threw it on the floor on top of her discarded top before he stood. "I've wanted to touch your chest every time you took off your shirt after our gym workouts." Reaching up, her fingertips traced the muscles of his shoulders down his chest to his abs. Her small palms grasped either side of his waist and pulled him closer. She nuzzled his belly with her nose and breathed deep before her tongue darted out, leaving a wet trail from his belly button to the waist of his pants. She tugged at the button until it came loose and unzipped his jeans. Her hands dipped into the back of his pants, pulling them down over his thighs with his boxers. Soft fingers grazed over his cock as he stepped out of his pants.

"Lean back," he whispered and knelt again.

She pushed back on her elbows, breasts peeking out, and her dark hair spilling over her shoulders. He flipped her hair out of the way and traced his fingers over her soft globes and along her ribs, following his fingers with his tongue until he reached her tattoo. "I've dreamed about getting up close and personal with this ever since you teased me with a glimpse."

Michelle giggled. "I didn't tease you."

His fingers traced the outline of a red rose. "Every time you reached above your head, a strip of skin showed at your waist and I'd get a peek at this." She shivered at his light touch. "I'd wonder exactly where the design ended."

"Now's your chance to find out." She wiggled out of her yoga pants, and he pulled them from her legs before getting a better look. The stem of the flower turned into an ivy pattern. It hooked over her hip and dipped into the soft, warm flesh of her lower abdomen.

"You know the inspiration of my tattoo. What does this represent?" he asked, tracing the flowing lines.

"Roses signify love, warmth, and resilience. The winding stem is life's twists and turns. Plus it's pretty badass, isn't it?" A sexy laugh bubbled from her throat.

"You are amazing," he said before inhaling the scent of her arousal. "I can't wait."

"Then what are you waiting for?" she asked, her eyelashes formed a sexy veil as the vivid blue of her eyes showed through.

Hunter growled and pulled his discarded jeans from the floor. Palming the pocket, he found his wallet and took a foiled square from the opening. Ripping it open, he sheathed his length and climbed over Michelle, leaning on his elbows on either side of her face.

He kissed her harder than he'd meant to, and she whimpered into his mouth and wrapped her legs around his waist, lifting her hips to meet his needy cock. He thrust into her warm folds, filling her to the hilt. She called out and he froze. "God, Michelle, you're so tight. Did I hurt you? Shit, I'm an ass. I'm sorry," he whispered and stroked her hair.

"Sorry?" A naughty grin formed on her face. "Make love to me, Hunter. Like it's our first time, our last time."

He knew what she needed because he desired the same thing. Her murmurs and pleas spurred him forward, every thrust, every groan spiraled them into the abyss of their passion. Her fingernails dragged down his slick back as he pumped into her. He hissed as she grabbed his ass. He was about to lose control. When he pulled out quickly, she moaned in protest. "Turn around, love."

He positioned her feet on the floor and leaned over her back as she bent over the bed. They moaned in unison as he pushed into her. He wouldn't be able to hold out long. His hand snaked around her hip and he ran his fingers up and down her folds, careful not to touch her most sensitive spot. She bucked her hips, meeting his thrusts.

"Please." Her hand covered his and guided him to her clit.

He bit back a throaty groan as she helped him bring her to the edge of her climax. He eased his length into her again, slow and deep. She let go of his hand and fisted the sheets and cried out his name. Cupping her sex, he buried his face into her hair and pumped his hips faster, driving them into a spiraling release. Moaning deep into the back of her neck, he eased her down onto the mattress. Her core pulsed, milking everything he had. He rolled onto his sweat slicked back. They lay spent in twisted sheets while catching their breath. He turned and studied her delicate features. Her hair flowed softly over her partially closed eyes. "Hey," he whispered, afraid he was too hard on her. Perhaps it was too much too soon.

Her eyes fluttered open and a smile appeared on her lips. "Hey yourself."

"You okay?"

"That was intense, incredible, and better than a hot fudge sundae with whipped cream." Her hand traveled over his belly and played with the hair on his chest. "I'm better than okay."

He gathered her into his arms and her back melded to his chest. "I'd never hurt you. Ever. I just can't control myself around you."

Michelle turned and straddled his hips. "I love that about you. About us."

He tugged at a lock of her hair and cupped her breasts. "Come here, baby. Let me taste you."

She leaned over and he took her nipple into his mouth. Flipping her over, she squealed as he threw her onto a sea of pillows. "What are you doing?"

"I promised to explore every inch of you, and that's what I intend to do. I'm a slow learner, sweetheart. This may take a while."

****

Michelle lay in his arms. They'd made love for hours, and she was physically and emotionally spent. However, her belly protested loudly. Her hands covered her stomach after the third loud growl.

He gave her a squeeze. "Hungry?"

"Yeah, I think we worked up an appetite. You did promise me dinner, remember?"

He laughed. "That's right. We never did get our date in, did we?"

"I guess that's a reason to see me again."

Hunter hunched up on his elbow and searched her eyes. His face held an expression she couldn't quite place. Or maybe she just didn't want to understand. His finger traced her lips. "How about I run to the corner and grab us a pizza with every imaginable topping?"

She nodded. "Sure, but no anchovies or onions. Everything else is fair game."

He rolled out of bed and threw on his clothes. "I'll be right back."

"Here, take these so you can let yourself back in." She reached for her purse on the floor, pulled out her key ring, and tossed it to him. He winked as he closed the door.

The room became cold and dreary as soon as Hunter left. She sat up and checked the time. It was past midnight. She rubbed her eyes. In a matter of hours, she'd confirmed what she'd known for a while. She was in love with a man she could never have. The smell of their passion lay heavy on her skin. Flipping the sheet from her legs, she padded into the bathroom and turned the knobs to fill her small bathtub. Besides the location, she'd loved that her apartment had a tub. Most studios were built with just a shower stall. Baths always put her at ease. She added a few drops of her favorite jasmine-scented bath oil, slipped into the steamy water, and closed her eyes.

She heard the lock turn on her door. "Pizza delivery for Miss Willis," he sung.

"I'm in here."

Hunter sauntered in and leaned against the door jam. "Forget the pizza, you look good enough to eat."

She wiggled a finger at him. "You're not tricking me with that line again, mister. Be a good deliveryman and bring me my pizza."

"I'll do better than that." He placed the box over the vanity sink and stripped off his clothes. Opening the lid, he pulled a slice out and moved to the bathtub. "Sit up."

She leaned forward and he stepped in behind her. As he sat, straddling her between his legs, the water came dangerously close to overflowing. She giggled and rested her back on his chest. "Now this is what I call service." He folded the pizza in half and held it to her mouth. Taking a large bite, she chewed the warm dough and cheese. "Mmm, so good. Thank you." They shared the slice, and Michelle leaned back into his chest and closed her eyes. "Can we just stay like this forever?"

"The water will probably get cold." He chuckled.

"How long?" Michelle asked without opening her eyes.

"I don't know. It's starting to get cold now, isn't it?" Hunter used his foot to turn the hot water knob. Steamy water slowly trickled from the faucet.

"You know what I mean."

His chest rose with a deep breath before falling as he let it out. "My flight leaves at noon."

Don't cry. Not now. She couldn't stop the single tear that landed on her cheek as she opened her eyes.

"Hey, come here." Hunter turned her around so she lay on his chest. He cupped her cheeks between his hands and wiped the tear with his thumb. "You're going to be okay."

Michelle swallowed hard. She didn't want him to see her fall apart. There'd be plenty of time for a full out breakdown after he was flying three thousand miles away from her. She met his stare. "I know, and so will you." She kissed him softly. "Make love to me again before you go."

Hunter brushed his lips across hers before nipping a trail along her bottom lip. She parted her mouth, and his tongue tangled with hers, searching, probing, wanting. Lifting her out of the tub like she weighed next to nothing, Hunter dried her off with a fuzzy towel and carried her to bed. He sat on the edge of the bed and ran his fingertip along her collarbone, in the valley between her breasts, and over her ribs. A small shiver ran through her body.

"Are you cold?" he asked.

She shook her head. "Don't stop."

Hunter leaned over, his lips capturing hers before leaving a trail of kisses along her jaw and down her neck. Caging her in with his elbows on either side of her head, he carefully climbed over her body. The heat of his skin radiated through her as she inhaled his scent, searing it to memory.

Hunter kissed his way down her stomach while holding her gaze. A warm line of sweet kisses headed toward the apex between her legs. Michelle groaned as his chin brushed her clit. "I found another one of your secrets."

"God yes, please don't stop."

A wicked smile formed on his lips as he draped her legs over his shoulders.

Michelle fisted her pillow as his tongue trailed a warm line up her sex. Moaning, he palmed the inner skin of her thighs, opening them to him. Her gaze stayed locked on him while his tongue dipped into her wet folds, slick with her desire. "Please. I want to feel you inside me."

"Not until I watch you come undone. Give me your hands."

She loosened the hold she had on the pillow and laid her hands by her sides. Hunter laced his fingers with hers as he continued his exploration of her heated sex. The tip of his tongue ran small circles around her clit. A throaty noise she didn't recognize escaped her mouth as waves of pleasure captured her body and wouldn't let go. She tightened the grip on his hand and called his name. Releasing one of her hands, he coaxed her climax with his fingers. Her orgasm touched every part of her. Hunter didn't relinquish until she was spent.

He crawled back up her body, careful not to crush her with his own weight. He kissed her hard, his tongue sharing the taste of her arousal. The taste of her essence on his mouth was more than she could take, and her sex flooded with warm juices once again.

"I want to feel you inside me. Taking what you need. Give me something to remember you."

Hunter rolled on a condom and pushed his length into her core, filling her completely. She wrapped her legs around him, vowing to keep him with her, even though she knew it was impossible. But for that night, which had quickly turned into morning, he was hers and hers alone. Sounds of their love filled her tiny studio until they shuttered in climax together.

Hunter rolled onto his side, taking Michelle with him, still inside her. He brushed the hair from her eyes, tucking it behind her ear before holding her to his chest. "Come with me."

"I thought I just did." She forced a giggle to try to lighten the mood—unsuccessfully.

"Come with me to California," he said, cupping her face and guiding her to meet his stare.

She took a breath and let it out slowly. "You don't mean that."

"I've never wanted anything in my life more than you. I need you with me. Come to Cali with me."

Michelle sat up. "How? I can barely make a living here."

He shrugged. "You can live with me. I'll take care of both of us."

Michelle placed her index finger to his lips. "Let's just lay here together for the time we have left." She closed her eyes and willed her tears away.

****

Michelle woke to Hunter's breath hot against the back of her head. He snaked an arm across her chest, wrapping her into a delicious embrace like a blanket right out of the dryer. Sweet. Warm. Right. She snuggled into his body. Her backside pressed against the heat of his erection.

"You're up," he whispered, his breath catching in his throat.

"No. I'm having the most amazing dream. Don't wake me up."

He pulled her in tighter. Normally any embrace would push her toward the nightmares that plagued her for so long. But the only thing she felt was safe.

He shifted and moved from her body, and instantly, cool air surrounded her. His palm rested on her shoulder and he nudged her around so she lay on her back, looking into her eyes, cradling her in warmth. She forced a smile. "Come. With. Me." His fingers caressed her shoulder, driving her further into the sexy cocoon known as Hunter McAvery.

She wanted to say yes. Pack her few things, and use the rest of her savings to buy a one-way ticket to California just to wake up with him every day. But fear took hold and captured her again. The what ifs outweighed the possibility of a future with Hunter. What if it didn't work out? What if it was his way of saying good-bye because he knew she wouldn't come? What if she was stuck in California with no money, no friends, or no job? What if she became a target again? What if he found out how screwed up she really was?

"I can't." Tears pooled in her eyes as she said those two words instead of what she really wanted to say.

"Why? I don't get it, Michelle. Like you said, you're barely making ends meet out here. What do you have to lose?"

Her job. Her security. Her peace of mind. The couple of friends she'd managed to keep. "This is my life, and I make it work. I can't just leave it to follow your dream. Please don't ask me to do that."

He searched her eyes, seemingly struggling with what to say. But after what seemed like an eternity, he nodded. "The offer is there. Please consider it. You—" He closed his mouth and shook his head.

"What?"

Hunter smiled, but his eyes were full of hurt. "You take care." He rolled over and sat up, scrubbing his face.

Turning to her side, Michelle surveyed his long, muscular body and studied the tattoo covering his arm and the morning scruff on his cheeks. She had to be crazy to let him leave her world.

He padded out of bed, collected his clothes from the floor, and trudged into the bathroom. Minutes later, he emerged as sexy as ever but with a shadowed look in his eyes. She sat up and hugged her knees to her chest. Hunter's smile seemed forced as he strode to the edge of the bed and sat next to her. "I have to go."

The words meant so many things. He had a flight to catch, but she knew he also meant he had to leave his life behind. New York and everything it stood for. Hunter was fighting demons too, and it was his way out.

"I need to stay," she said, and they both knew was a lie. She could throw caution to the wind and go. Try. Her mother used to say "nothing ventured is nothing earned." It was the saying that made her attempt to pick up the pieces after graduation and move to the busiest city she could think to move to. That was a gamble. She could take a gamble again. However, all of the "what ifs" kept running through her head.

"I know." He brushed her temple with the pad of his fingers and tucked a strand of hair behind her ear. Reaching over, he slanted his mouth over hers.

Her lips melded to his as her hand trailed up his arm, memorizing the feel of his skin. Reaching his neck, she pulled him closer in a feeble attempt to capture his warmth and keep it with her forever. She whimpered in his mouth as he pulled away.

"I'm sorry."

She nodded. There were so many words left unspoken. So much she wanted to tell him. She opened her mouth but closed it again. There was no use. "Me too." It was all she could say.

Hunter stood and sauntered to the door. Her vision blurred as he walked out of her life. Opening the door, he rested his forehead on the surface and turned his head toward her. The pain in his eyes equaled the crush of her heart.

"Knock 'em dead in Cali," she said with a forced smile.

Opening the door farther, he left without another glance, without another word.

Michelle closed her eyes as the soft click sounded and the muffled footsteps disappeared. The normal sounds of her apartment took over her senses as Hunter left her world forever. She was alone. Again. But this time it was her choice, and she sobbed into the pillow, wondering how it was the right one. Reaching over to her bedside table, she removed the pill bottle she hadn't touched in months and tipped the bottle. Three pills slid out. One more than she normally took. Popping them into her mouth, she shuffled to the kitchen and filled a glass of water. Gulping them, down she trudged back to bed and sank her head into the pillow, waiting for the effects to take over.

Before everything went cloudy, she remembered the door remained unlocked, and a shiver passed through her body. She was exposed. Pulling the blanket from her bed, she wrapped it around her shoulders and stood. Wobbling on unsteady legs, she walked a wavy line to the door. Her vision blurred as she turned the locks. She turned to head back to bed when darkness enclosed her body. The dark. For a moment, terror immobilized her and she froze. However, fear only lasted a moment before the medication kicked in, and she drifted off into nothingness.

****

The ringing hurt her brain as it continued, stopped, and started again. Her eyes fluttered open and a searing pain washed over her back, registering in her cloudy brain. She was leaning against her door wrapped in her blanket. Blinking, her gaze moved to her window. Afternoon shadows filled her apartment. Her phone chimed, indicating a message was left.

Michelle tried to stand, but the pain in her head wouldn't allow it. She crawled to her bed and found her phone lying on the floor. Swiping the screen with one hand, she held her head up with the other as she leaned on her bed. Five missed calls from Hunter and seven from Miranda. *Shit*. She was hours late for work. Ignoring the messages, she called Miranda.

She answered after the first ring. "Are you okay?"

"Yeah. I'm okay." Michelle hardly recognized her own voice.

"You don't sound okay, little one. Where are you? I tried to ring your buzzer and no answer. I was about to call the police."

"I'm in my apartment. I overslept. I'm sorry. Will be right down."

"I don't care about you missing work. I'm worried about you. I'll be over as soon as Cheyenne gets in."

"Really, I'm fine. Don't come." Michelle glanced at her reflection and barely recognized the person staring back at her. No amount of makeup would camouflage the dark circles under her bloodshot eyes. "In fact, I might be coming down with something. I don't want you to catch it."

The silence on the other end seemed to go on forever. "You're sure you're okay? You can tell me anything. You know that, don't you?"

"I know, and yes, I'll be fine." She nodded to convince herself as much as Miranda.

"Take the rest of the day off and get some rest. If you're feeling better tomorrow, come in so we can talk. I'll stop over with some dinner for you on my way home from the gallery."

"No." The word came out more forceful than she had intended. "Thanks, Miranda, but I have plenty of food here." Her voice softened as another lie flowed freely from her mouth. "I'll be in tomorrow."

"All right. But if you're not here tomorrow, I'm coming by whether you like it or not."

"Okay."

"Rest up, little one."

Michelle poked at the screen until the call disconnected and powered down her phone, avoiding a call from the other caller. He was gone for good, and no amount of words exchanged on a cross-country call could change the fact that he chose to put distance between them. She had two choices: curl up and cry, or move on with her life. Michelle made a deal with herself: one pity day complete with polishing off the pint of emergency pistachio ice cream she kept in the back of her tiny freezer. Then, she'd wake up, shower, put on her best face, and get on with her life.

She'd survived other losses. A broken heart would be a piece of cake. She was a survivor. She'd survive. She had to, because there was no alternative.

COLORS OF US

Chapter Eighteen

A ringtone woke Michelle from a deep sleep. *Damn it.* She squinted as she felt around for her phone. She'd hoped she hadn't overslept. It hadn't happened since making the stupid decision to take those pills after Hunter left three weeks ago. She dumped the rest of them in the trash shortly after. Picking up her phone, she blinked at the display. The Locke Gallery's phone number flashed on her phone as she glanced at the time. It was only seven.

She swiped her finger over the screen. "Hello?"

"Get down here, little one. I have big news for you, and I have to tell you in person."

"Miranda? What are you doing at the gallery so early?"

"Don't ask me questions. Just get down here pronto, girl."

The call disconnected and Michelle laid the phone on the blanket. What had Miranda so fired up? Maybe she acquired one of the A-list artists to show their work at the gallery. Michelle smiled at Miranda's excitement.

Pulling herself out of bed, she showered and threw on a pair of yoga pants and a sweatshirt and headed downstairs. Michelle turned the handle of the building's front door and stuck her hand out to check the weather. A gust of wind prickled at her skin, and she decided to jog the ten blocks instead of taking her bike. It was the perfect running temperature. Sliding on her gloves, she strapped her backpack on and headed toward the gallery. The sound of her footsteps helped her focus on taking deep breaths in through her nose and out through her mouth.

She ran until she crossed the street to the gallery's block and glanced up at Primo Java. Peering through the window confirmed the coffee business was booming. Michelle hadn't been back into the shop since having coffee with Hunter. Her gaze moved to the table they'd occupied. It seemed like a much longer period of time had passed since meeting him. So much had happened in her life. She'd even sold a few more pieces, resulting in extra cash, allowing her to splurge on fancy coffee once in a while. She pulled open the door and walked in, enjoying the rich smell of dark coffee tickling at her nose as she shuffled into the line. It didn't take her long to reach the barista at the other side of the counter.

"Two lattes, please."

"Anything else, miss?"

Her eyes wandered to the pastry case and zeroed in on the pile of peanut butter chocolate chip cookies. "One of those, too." She pointed to the plate.

Chuckling to herself at the ease of spending twelve hard-earned dollars on non-necessities such as gourmet coffee and a cookie, Michelle justified the expense as a way of celebrating whatever made Miranda wake up and go to the gallery so early.

Taking a sip of her coffee, she strode the rest of the block to Locke Gallery. As she approached the gallery's window, she knew something was missing. Her portrait was removed from the wall. Nodding, she figured Miranda's new artist requested the space. Fair enough. Michelle had used the prime wall space for far too long. She'd probably be relegated to a wall in the back. Michelle forced a fake smile and pulled open the gallery door.

"There you are. What took you so long to get down here?" Miranda asked and gave her a quick hug. "One of these for me? Bless you child."

Michelle handed her a cup. "I bought us a cookie too. So what's this all about?" She tried not to stare at her self-portraits leaning against the desk and the box of packing paper alongside the paintings.

"I thought you'd want to take a look at them before they get picked up." Miranda folded her arms and smiled.

"Picked up? What are you talking about?" Her heartbeat sped up as her gaze moved from the paintings to Miranda.

"Michelle Willis, you just made your first collection sale. Full price." Miranda clapped before hugging Michelle and patting her back.

Michelle pulled back and widened her eyes. "Full price? Are you kidding me?" Out of love for the paintings, she'd priced them twice as much as they were worth on the market. Calculating the prices she remembered assigning, she came up with an amount that was more than she ever thought she'd make on her paintings in a lifetime. "Who? When?"

"The call came in yesterday, and I finally reached the buyer's agent last night. I wanted to be sure it was for real before telling you about it. The funds hit the bank account about an hour ago, and a messenger service will be here to pick them up soon."

Michelle sat on the floor next to the largest painting in her likeness. She studied the image's eyes. There was so much sadness in those eyes, but the colors in her hair glowed bright against the darkness of her expression. Michelle was that woman at one time. She was a shell of a person trying desperately to break free of the prison of guilt and torment.

A warm touch to her shoulder brought her back to the present. "Are you ready to give them up?" Miranda asked, crouching next to Michelle. "You're not the same person anymore, you know."

Michelle nodded. "I'm ready."

"Good, because they're already sold and there's no way we're giving the money back."

Michelle giggled. "I don't get it. I don't remember anyone in here who seemed remotely interested enough to buy them."

Miranda picked up one the smaller canvases and placed it on the pile of paper. "Don't question it. When it comes to art, images dig in and hook the buyer. When a painting talks to you, you're just snagged. We're lucky the person you snagged has the cash to lay down for it. Things are going to change for you now."

Michelle shook her head and wrapped up the one of the large canvases. "I don't think so."

Miranda set the painting down and turned to Michelle. Cupping her face, Miranda forced her to meet her stare. "It's time to spread your wings and move on, little one. You've come too far to retreat back into your shell and watch life pass you by."

Michelle scanned the gallery. "But this is where I belong."

"Not anymore," Miranda whispered and dropped her hand from Michelle's face.

Searching her eyes, Michelle stared at the only person who believed in her when no one else did. "You don't want me here?"

Miranda chuckled and took Michelle into her arms. "You're like a daughter to me, and I wish I could keep you here forever, but it's time. You're destined for great things. You have a promising career as an artist, not to mention there's someone who's wickedly in love with you. Go hard and fast after both of them. You'll regret it forever if you don't."

Pulling out another sheet of paper, Michelle set the smallest painting in the middle and covered it. "Love is a strong word. If he loved me, why did he leave?"

"Hunter left to make a clean break from memories that continued to haunt him here. I remember the accident. It happened just a few blocks from here. I'd never met Hunter before he came in here for you. When Alex and I were together, Hunter was still at school. Alex used to say Hunter was going to be a great businessman with a houseful of kids. He seemed to be the direct opposite of Alex. He was engaged to his college sweetheart. The plan was for him to finish graduate school before they got married. Alex called him an old soul. I wondered how the accident was going to affect Hunter. Then he started working for Alex and following in his footsteps, and I figured that's how he was going to cope with his loss. I just didn't want you to get caught up in his issues, little one. That's not what I wanted for you." She tapped her index finger on Michelle's nose. "But what I didn't bank on is you two helping to heal each other. I'd bet this gallery he's hurting as much as you are right now. Go to him. What do you have to lose?"

Michelle choked back a sob. "Everything. My job. My home. You."

Miranda reached out and tucked a lock of hair behind Michelle's ear. "You always have me. You can return anytime. But now it's time to find out where you belong."

Michelle smiled and finished packing her paintings to be picked up. Touching each one, she looked at Miranda. "I'm gonna take a walk." She didn't want to watch her work as it left the gallery.

The air was colder than earlier that day as she stepped outside. She found herself zigzagging though the city streets, heading for the park and the koi pond. After

Hunter left, she took over the responsibility of feeding the fish. Walking briskly to the park's entrance, she heard her name over the howling wind.

"Michelle! Michelle!"

She turned toward the woman's voice and spotted Jacey waving as she crossed the street.

"I thought that was you." Jacey gave her a hug and rubbed her bare hands together. "I didn't realize it would be so cold today."

"It got worse. Are you on your way to work?"

"Yeah. I'm a little early, though. Where are you headed?"

"Into the park to feed Hunter's fish," she said matter-of-factly.

"His fish? In the park?" Jacey gave her a confused look.

Michelle laughed. "Why don't you grab a hot cup of coffee over there and join me?"

"Okay, you piqued my interest." Jacey strode into a coffee shop and returned with two steaming cups. "And just how far away are these fish of Hunter's?" Jacey cocked an eyebrow.

"Not far at all. Just around the bend over there."

The women walked until the pond was in view. "How did Hunter, and now you, become the responsible party for these fish?"

Michelle recounted the story of the first fish and how he came to collect all of them. She also realized Jacey didn't know Hunter moved to LA.

"So he really did it? He really moved out. That took a lot of courage. It's too bad that you two never got together." She shrugged, and Michelle continued to throw bits of bread into the water and watch them float until the morsels were eaten up or sunk to the bottom. "Wait a minute. You did get together. Didn't you?"

"Why do you say that?"

"Because you won't look at me, and your face is turning red."

"Not that it matters now, but we did 'get together,' as you say, before he left for California."

"No kidding? Actually, I had no idea but figured I'd call your bluff."

Michelle laughed and swatted Jacey on the arm. "I want details."

"A girl doesn't kiss and tell. But I think I love him, Jace."

"Shit. Falling for a McAvery isn't easy. Look at what happened to me. But Hunter is different than Alex. He had it bad for you. From the moment he saw your portrait in the window, he had to have you."

Michelle's eyes widened. "Oh my God."

"What?"

"Someone just bought my entire collection for a huge sum of money. Do you think Hunter would've done that?"

"I don't think he has the resources for that sort of thing. His bastard of a brother, well, that's another story."

****

Michelle scanned the bar as memories of Hunter flooded back. Nothing had changed except the person on the other side of the bar. Instead of muscular, shaggy-haired, tattooed, sexy-as-all-hell Hunter McAvery, there stood a young, gangly guy Michelle remembered as the stock boy. Alex must've given him a shot at bartending. He nodded at her as she approached the bar.

"Is Alex here?"

"No, but he's on his way in. Want something while you wait?"

Michelle slipped onto a barstool. "Diet soda with lemon, please." She turned to the wall she'd spent so much time focusing on and examined her work. Every table, every corner, and every face in the painting told a story. She hadn't really looked and appreciated the work that went into the mural until that moment.

Cool air poured into the bar as the door opened. A familiar voice called over the hum of the bar patrons as he greeted the staff. Michelle swiveled on her stool and waved, and Alex's face lit up with a smile as he strode to her spot at the bar. "Michelle, to what does McAvery's owe the honor of your presence?"

Michelle narrowed her eyes. "I think you know."

"How about we go into my office and you can enlighten me?" Alex held out his hand and guided Michelle to his office. "Take a seat," he said, closing the door. "What's on your mind?"

"My self-portrait collection sold at full price. That never happens to unknown artists like me."

Alex raised his brows. "Maybe your work caught the eye of some rich art collector."

"Possible, but not probable. I first thought of Hunter, but I don't think he has that kind of money. Then you came to mind as the next educated guess. Don't lie to me, Alex. I need to know if it was you, and if so, I need to know why."

He took a deep breath and leaned on the corner of his desk. "I am the buyer, but it had nothing to do with Hunter. I promise. He has no idea I bought it."

Relief set in with his promise Hunter wasn't involved. The last thing she wanted was to be manipulated into moving to California to be with him. "Why did you buy it?"

"First and foremost, I like it. It's a fantastic collection. The second reason is hard to explain."

"Try. I need to hear it."

Alex walked to the other side of the desk and sunk into his chair. He suddenly looked tired as he rubbed his eyes and scrubbed his hands down his face like Hunter occasionally did. "Your self-portraits portray every woman I've dated and dropped over the years."

"You mean every woman whose heart you've broken?"

"Yes. I'm a jerk, Michelle. I know I am, but I want to change. I think buying your collection will help me change."

"I'm not sure I follow you."

"The sadness and beauty in the expressions of those portraits remind me of what I do to women. Your collection hanging on my wall will be a constant reminder to break that cycle."

"You're a good person, Alex. But you need to break down the wall you built around you and allow yourself to be vulnerable."

"Like you did with Hunter."

A lump caught in her throat hearing his name. "How is he?"

"He's worried about you. Why won't you take his calls?"

Hunter's number flashed on her screen too many times to count over the past few weeks. She didn't want his pity. She deleted every message he left. What was done was done. Nothing could change the fact that he now lived across the country. "He told you?"

Alex smiled. "He really wants to talk to you, but I think I know what he'd like better."

"And what would that be?"

He reached for her hand and squeezed her palm. "To see you. You'd love California."

COLORS OF US

Chapter Nineteen

Hunter glanced out his office window at the setting sun of another beautiful California Friday afternoon. He'd fallen in love with the weather. His office was less than a mile from the ocean, and he spent many late afternoons walking the beach. He bought a second-hand surfboard and looked forward to trying it out over the weekend.

"Hey, a bunch of us are heading to Smokey's for drinks after work. Join us, and we won't fall for your lame excuses this time," his coworker, Jim, said from the threshold of his office. He had successfully dodged a few drinks after work invitations over the past couple of weeks with excuses ranging from unpacking to waiting for a furniture delivery.

Hunter rubbed his eyes and looked blearily at his coworker.

"You look like you can use some fun, man. I won't take no for an answer. Come on, I'll introduce you to the locals."

Hunter rolled his eyes. The last invitation came with a promise of meeting a few local chicks. Hunter had had his fill of chicks. He was sure California women weren't much different than New York women. The thought of it made him cringe. The only person he wanted was hiding in New York City, too headstrong to leave her comfort zone. Whoever heard of hiding in New York, anyway? He stopped calling her every day. Her silence was an indication that she wanted him out of her life. He thought about calling Cheyenne at the gallery and ask how she was but decided against the idea. Instead, he asked Alex to check on her.

"Yeah, a drink sounds good. I'll meet you there. I have to run home first. My brother sent me something that's supposed to be delivered today. I want to pick it up so it's not sitting by the door too long." Alex had texted him a vague message earlier to tell him to be home after work for a delivery.

"All right, we'll see you down there. Don't bail on me."

Hunter gave him a salute and powered down his computer. "I'll be there. I can use a cold beer today." It'd be nice to be served at a bar instead of being the one serving. It was time he started doing more than work. Work had kept his mind off Michelle and contacting Liam. It was a shitstorm he wasn't ready to face just yet.

Hunter changed into a T-shirt, pair of shorts, and running shoes and stuffed his work clothes into a backpack. Since moving to California, he took up running to help clear his mind and learn the neighborhoods around his office. He had three months to find a place to live while staying in the company-owned condominium. His dream house would be near the beach, and he was drawn to the artist colony area of Laguna. Michelle had awakened many things within him, one being an appreciation of art. He spent his Sunday mornings wandering around the streets of Laguna Beach, window-shopping the galleries. It'd somehow made him feel closer to Michelle, even though pain sliced through him knowing he'd never have her.

Hunter sprinted the last half mile to his apartment. Causing his body pain and discomfort helped ease the constant gut-wrenching pain he felt when he thought about Michelle and the last night they shared. Moving to California didn't help him escape thoughts of her and the anguish of not being able to hold her in his arms. He could still feel the warmth of her skin on his fingertips.

He raced up the stairs of the building, taking two steps at a time, and glanced around the small entryway. No package from Alex. Pulling his phone from his backpack, he found Alex's number and pushed Send. One ring, then another buzzed in his ear. On the fourth ring, Hunter was about to hang up when the call was answered. Music and laughter filled his ear. He pulled the phone from his ear to check if he had the right phone number. Glancing at the display, he heard Alex's voice.

"Hello? Hello? Hunter?"

"Yeah, it's me. What, are you having a party there without me?" He yelled into the phone.

"Shit, I can barely hear you. It's the night of the Fall Fling Crawl. How soon you forget!"

Alex was right. Hunter's new life was far from New York's annual bar crawls. "That's right. I won't keep you, but I wanted to ask you about the delivery."

Alex laughed, and Hunter wasn't sure if it was focused at him or someone at the bar. "I'm glad you like it. You deserve it, Hunt. Hey, I'll talk to you Sunday, okay?"

Alex hung up before Hunter could ask him about the mysterious missing package.

****

Michelle's heart beat hard in her chest as the cab made a right on Forsythia Place. She glanced at the slip of paper Alex had scrawled Hunter's address on: 2532 Forsythia Place. She peered at the numbers on the rows of townhouses as the driver pulled along the curb next to a white structure appearing to be a low-rise walkup apartment building.

"This is it, miss. Comes to thirty-five dollars," the driver said, glancing at her in the rearview mirror.

Michelle pulled a few bills from her wallet and handed it over the seat. "Do me a favor and stay here for a few minutes."

The cabbie examined the money, he nodded and he turned off the engine before getting out of the cab and pulling her suitcase from the trunk. He opened the back door. "I'll wait five minutes."

Taking a deep breath, she stretched her legs and slid out of the cab. "Thanks."

As she pulled the handle from the suitcase, footsteps sounded behind her. Turning, she glanced at a young blonde woman strutting up the stairs to Hunter's apartment with a champagne bottle in her hand. Long, tan legs glowed in contrast to her black skirt and what appeared to be at least four-inch heels. She was a typical California girl who could've walked straight out of a fashion magazine. Glancing down at her rumpled jeans and ballerina flats, Michelle felt most unglamorous in comparison. Watching the woman press one of the apartment's doorbells, she smoothed her hair as she checked her reflection in the front door's window.

"Hello?" a husky voice answered. A voice Michelle knew well.

"Hey, Hunter. It's me," the woman said with a smile.

A buzzer sounded, and she pushed open the door, her high heels clicking on the entryway floor. Tears blurred Michelle's vision as the door slammed shut. How stupid could she be to think Hunter was pining over her in the land of beautiful women? She remembered what Cheyenne said about Hunter and Alex the day she met Hunter in the coffee shop. *The McAvery brothers are playboys. They play the field and break hearts along the way.* Hunter always discounted those types of remarks, saying it was Alex's reputation and people thought he was guilty by association.

Alex McAvery. It was his fault she'd flown three thousand miles to a man who obviously didn't want her. Blinking back tears, she wished she had never met the McAverys.

She pulled her bag back to the cab and slapped the hood of the trunk. "Open, please."

The cabbie jumped and swung open his door. "That was quick. Where to now, miss?"

"Back to the airport."

He shrugged and hoisted her suitcase into the trunk.

****

Hunter cringed at Courtney's fake nails tapping on his door. He knew something was up when Jim called to tell him she was on her way over because she needed a ride to Smokey's. Courtney was one of the trainees at the firm and had been overly friendly with Hunter since his first day on the job. He had just gotten out of the shower when he received the phone call, and the buzz at the door a few minutes later, led Hunter to believe it was a planned setup.

He quickly pulled on a pair of jeans and a T-shirt; his hair was still wet and dripping onto his shoulders. He was about to ask her to wait for him outside but figured that would be rude, and he did have to work with her.

He swung open the door. "Hey Courtney. Give me a second to finish getting dressed. You can wait over there," Hunter said, pointing to his sofa.

"No hurry. In fact, I thought we could hang out a little before heading over to Smokey's. I brought a bottle of champagne to celebrate." She giggled as she held the bottle up and cocked her head.

He raised his eyebrows. "Celebrate? What are we celebrating?"

"How about your move to California and starting a new job. Does one really need a reason to celebrate? You seem kind of lonely, Hunter. I'll bet no one welcomed you properly."

Lonely. Yeah, he was lonely. But not for the kind of company Courtney offered. She had already moved to his kitchenette and was searching his cabinets for glasses, which he didn't have. Shrugging, she grabbed two plastic cups from the stack next to his sink and unwrapped the top of the bottle.

"That's okay. I don't drink—"

The cork popped and hit the hanging light fixture over the counter. "Oops. Sorry." She giggled again and poured the cups to the rim, making Hunter inwardly cringe.

"Why don't you start without me? I'm going to finish getting dressed." Hunter pointed to his bedroom.

"Hold on. I have a toast." She picked up both cups and handed one to Hunter, spilling drops of champagne on the counter.

He stepped forward and took the cup from her. "Okay, go ahead."

"To your success in California, the land of dreams. May all of yours come true." Courtney held her cup to him.

"The land of dreams? I thought it was the land of overpriced real estate. You know what they want for a two-bedroom house around here?" He tipped his cup to hers and placed it on the counter.

She giggled loud and gulped half of the contents of her cup. "You're funny, Hunter. This is a nice apartment. Want to show me around?"

His feet stayed planted in his kitchenette. "There's not much to see. Living room, bedroom, bathroom." He pointed toward the location of each.

Courtney smiled and strode around the living room. She peeked into the bedroom before slowly approaching him and setting her cup on the counter next to his. "Look, if you haven't noticed, I'm coming on to you."

He nodded. "Don't take this the wrong way, you're beautiful and sweet, but I'm just not interested. I'm sorry."

Her face flushed. "Wow. This is embarrassing." She picked up her cup and tipped back the rest of the champagne.

Hunter's phone sounded from the bedroom and he lifted his index finger. "One second," he mouthed and left her in the kitchenette. He found his phone on his dresser flashing Alex's number. He swiped the screen. "Hey."

"What the hell are you doing, Hunter?"

"What are you talking about?"

"I told you a surprise was being delivered, and you bring a girl to your apartment?" Alex yelled.

"What? How did you know?" Hunter looked around like he was being watched. "What's going on?"

"Dude. Michelle was there. She came to surprise you, and before she could even get to your door, you invite some blonde in."

Hunter slammed his hand on the dresser. "Michelle was here? When? Where is she now?"

"You blew it, bro. She's on her way back to the airport. She's probably there right now, trying to get a flight back to New York. You hurt her. If I had known you were already seeing women out there, I never would've told her to go. I thought you loved her."

"I did. I do love her. This is all a misunderstanding. Shit. I need to stop her."

"Better move fast, Hunt."

Hunter ended the call and scrolled through his contacts, looking for Michelle's number. Pressing send, he groaned when his call went right to her voice mail. "Michelle. Please, baby. Don't leave. What you saw was nothing. It's a misunderstanding. Please call me back." Ending the call, he threw his phone on the dresser and rested his palms on the edge looking at his face in the mirror. *You really fucked things up this time, McAvery.*

"Is everything all right?" Courtney called from the door.

He just let the woman he loved more than anything in the world slip through his fingers.

"Hunter?"

He turned to see the concerned look on Courtney's face. "Sorry. I have to go." He strode to the door and turned the knob. "Just turn the lock on your way out," he said before slipping out the door.

He raced up to the next block where he parked the old Chevy Nova he bought from a used car lot the day he arrived in California. Jumping in, he turned the key in the ignition and shifted the gear stick to drive. He hit the gas pedal and steered the car toward the freeway. Hoping for an open road, his prayers went unanswered when he drove into bumper-to-bumper traffic.

"Shit." He smacked the steering wheel and pulled the phone from his pocket. Redialing Michelle's number, his call went to her voice mail again.

It felt as though he could've crawled to LAX faster than it took him to drive. His only hope was Michelle's cab hitting the same amount of traffic. He finally turned onto the exit ramp to the airport entrance. Taking a guess at which airline she was flying, he headed toward terminal parking. He was tempted to pull into the departure area and leave his car but decided to do the right thing. Somehow bad decisions seemed to plague him lately. Making a turn into short term parking, he scanned the sea of parked cars. He passed other cars trolling for parking spots and rode up the ramps to the highest and least crowded parking deck. After taking a deep breath and sending a prayer to anyone who'd listen, Hunter raced down the stairs and into the airport to the nearest departures board.

Scanning the city names, he came to the next flight leaving for New York's LaGuardia Airport. If that was the flight she was on, he had just under an hour to find Michelle. The logical thing would be to try to retrace her steps. He took a quick walk around the ticket counters but figured she'd already passed through the section to get her ticket. That left security and the waiting area at the gate, and he'd need a ticket to gain access to inside the terminal. The chance was small, but he decided to scan the line of passengers waiting at the security check-in before purchasing a ticket. He found the line she would've waited in and stood next to the roped area on tiptoes, looking for her dark hair.

"Can I help you?"

Hunter turned toward the voice of a security agent checking tickets. "No. Just looking for someone."

"You can't stand here, sir."

"Hold on. I just—" He spotted the back of her head. "Michelle! Michelle!"

She turned around and the sadness in her eyes punched him in the gut. She shook her head and turned to face the line.

"Shit," he grumbled. "Michelle, baby. Please. I need to talk to you."

"Sir, I said you can't stand here without a ticket."

"Michelle!"

She turned around again, glaring. Damn, she was beautiful when she was angry. She held her index finger up to the woman in back of her and said something to her before dodging people in line, heading in his direction. Standing on the other side of the rope, she pointed her finger to his chest. "Go home, Hunter. I don't need your pity. It was stupid for me to come out here. Please don't embarrass me more than I am already and just go home."

"Sweetheart, you have it all wrong."

"The only thing wrong was to come all the way out here. Good-bye, Hunter." Her hand moved from his chest. A shiver passed through his body as she turned from him and returned to her place in line.

"Fuck." His fist came down hard on one of the stands holding up the security line markers. The agent reached for his radio, and Hunter knew if he continued to draw attention to himself, he'd be detained and locked in some interrogation room while Michelle boarded a plane and left his life forever. He held up his hand. "Okay, no problem. I'm leaving."

The agent replaced the radio and nodded.

Hunter swung around and raced to the counter and bought a ticket to New York, hoping it was the same flight she was on. At least he would be able to talk to her in the terminal, and if she wouldn't talk to him, he would follow her back to New York. Nothing mattered anymore but getting her back.

He rushed back to the security line and flipped his driver's license from his wallet, showing both documents to the agent, who nodded him through. The line crawled forward as he checked his watch for what seemed like the millionth time in ten minutes. He had just less than thirty minutes to find her and talk her into staying before boarding the flight.

Security agents stopped him for an extra check. "It's standard when purchasing a ticket during the same day as travel," they explained as they patted him down.

Finally! He was cleared and free to find her in the crowded terminal.

He had to get her back. Seeing her again filled the ache in his heart. He told himself he'd left New York to run toward his dream, but in reality, he was running away. Running away from his past and any future of finding love. This was his chance to get her back, and failure wasn't an option. Luck was finally on his side when he spotted her sitting at the flight gate to New York's La Guardia Airport.

Chapter Twenty

Michelle rubbed her temples. If he was with another woman, why would he follow her to the airport? Guilt? He was caught and felt guilty she'd traveled across the country to see him. Nothing made sense. Tears filled her eyes when he pleaded with her at the security stop. She didn't know what to think.

"Michelle!" a breathy voice called, and she turned to see Hunter coming up fast, panting.

She stood and grabbed her bag to stand near the doors to the gate. "Hunter, what are you doing?"

He stopped and leaned against a pillar, huffing and puffing. "Give me a chance to explain."

Her gaze moved to the ticket in his hand, and she narrowed her eyes. "You bought a ticket?"

"I did, and I'm not going to leave you alone until you hear what I have to say. If you won't listen to me now, I'm going to follow you back to New York."

Michelle shook her head and willed her eyes to stay dry. "I don't know why I came. I don't blame you for moving on. I should've too. Just let me go back home." She stood to walk away, but Hunter stepped in front of her, blocking her path. Her gaze trailed down his chest and settled on his tattoo. He'd developed a slight tan over the past few weeks, which brought out the vivid reds and blue hues of the design.

"Please, just hear me out. If you listen to what I have to say, I'll leave. I'll go back home if that's what you want. I only ask that you listen."

She searched his eyes. Damn, she missed him. "Look. No explanation is necessary. It was stupid to come all the way out here. You moved for a reason. To get away from New York and everything in it. Including me."

"I asked you to come with me. Remember? I know what it looked like back there at my apartment, but it was hardly the case. Please sit down and hear me out. Please."

"Flight 934 will board in ten minutes. Please have your boarding passes ready."

Michelle raised her eyebrows. "Looks like we have ten minutes." she said and led him to a couple of free seats. Her skin warmed when her leg brushed against his as she sat. She had to stay strong. She crossed her arms. "Go ahead."

Hunter knelt on the floor and gazed into her eyes.

"Hunter, get up. People are staring at us."

"Let them." He took her hand into his. "Meeting you was the best thing that happened to me in a long time. Probably ever. I don't blame you for wanting to stay away from me. But I can't stay away from you, at least not until I try everything to get you back. You're all I could think about the past few weeks. I know you saw a coworker walk into my apartment. But that's what she is. A coworker. The guys I work with have tried to get me to go out for drinks with them. I finally agreed to go, and Courtney showed up at my apartment for a ride to the club. That's why she was there. It was for a ride."

"I'm not an idiot. I saw her primping herself in the reflection of the window. I know when a girl is flirting. Something tells me it's not as simple as that."

Hunter nodded and blew out a breath. "You're right, it wasn't. But nothing happened. I told her there was someone else. Damn it, Michelle, don't you get it?"

Michelle felt the eyes of a few nearby nosy passengers. "Let's take a walk."

Hunter stood and held his hand out for her.

Refusing to take his hand, she stood and walked ahead of him. She pointed to an empty corner of the gate, and he followed her to the semi-private section. She spun around and glared at him. "Look, I'll lay it on the line for you, because I'm tired and I can't fight anymore. Ready?"

"Give it to me."

She crossed her arms and leaned against the wall. "Here it is. Look at your coworker and look at me. There's a big difference. She's all bubbly and blonde, and I'm—" Michelle reached out with both hands to her side and slapped her jean covered legs. "I'm just not. I'll never be like that. You're on the fast track to succeed in corporate America. You need a girl like that at your side."

"You were ready to do it, though, weren't you? By coming out to California. You were ready to give it a try."

"I was talked into it. Miranda thought it was the best thing to find out if I belonged here. It took me all of one minute to see that I don't."

"You're wrong. You are so wrong and are selling yourself short. If I wanted someone like Courtney, do you think I had to come all the way to California to find her? There were a million Courtneys in New York."

Michelle thought back to Samantha and realized he wasn't interested in her either. "So what do you want," she whispered.

Hunter closed the space between them and ran his fingers through her hair, pulling a knot gently as his hand glided down to her shoulder. The tip of his index finger traced her jawbone until it reached her chin. He hooked his finger under and guided her face to meet his stare. The pad of his thumb traced her lips and she parted her mouth. She craved his touch and her insides melted with each swipe of his finger.

"Isn't it obvious? I haven't stopped thinking about you since the moment I got here. It scared me to think I lost you—" His adam's apple bobbled as he swallowed hard. "I never felt this way about anyone. Even before. Even with Isabel." He closed his eyes. "I'm an ass for saying that, aren't I? She's fucking dead because of me."

"No. She's dead because of a horrible accident. You didn't mean for it to happen, and you need to stop letting it eat you up inside."

"I can say the same thing about you. You're letting your fear rule your life."

Michelle nodded. "That was true even a few months ago, but not anymore. I want to live and trust and love." Michelle looked away and stared out the window, her eyes following a cart loaded with suitcases pull up to an airplane as she wiped a tear from her cheek.

Hunter closed the space between them with his body and wiped a tear from her cheek before tucking her hair behind her ear. "You can start by living, trusting, and loving me, sweetheart. We're meant to be together. You can't deny what we have. I want to tell you something I never said to you before."

She met his stare. "What?"

"Your self-portrait. It helped me."

She tried to hide her smile. "I painted it at a really bad time in my life. It was a combination of what I was feeling and what I wanted to feel."

"There was something about your eyes that... I know this is going to sound weird, but they understood what I was going through. They knew my pain."

Michelle turned to face the window. "I do know, or at least I understand it."

His presence warmed her back as strong arms wrapped around her. His breath blew heavy on her hair. "Stay with me." His breath caught as he whispered in her ear. "Please, I can't do this without you."

Tears washed over her face and dripped to the back of her hand as her palm covered his fingers. "I'm afraid."

"No. You're not afraid anymore. You're brave and beautiful, and you're going to be just fine. We both will."

She turned in his arms and searched his eyes. He cupped her face into his hands, wiping the tears with his thumbs. "You sound pretty confident about that."

"I am. I have to be. We have no other choice. Stay. Please. I can't lose you again."

Michelle nodded, and her gaze focused on his lips. She'd wanted to kiss him from the minute she saw him at the security line making a fool out of himself. She pushed up onto her tiptoes and his lips crashed down on hers. Gathering her into his arms, his tongue eased past her lips. She whimpered into his mouth, relaxing her muscles, letting him take over, giving herself to the man she trusted would help heal her and make her whole. She ran her fingers through his hair and scrubbed her other hand over the planes of his stubbled cheek, taking in his taste and smell. Nudging her backward, he sandwiched her between the wall and his muscular chest. Feeling the growing evidence of his arousal on her belly, her nipples tightened under her bra.

She broke their kiss. "We'd better get out of here before we're thrown out," she whispered into his ear. Looking over his shoulder, she caught the knowing eye of a few passengers sitting close to where they stood.

"Let's go." Hunter wrapped his arm around her shoulder as they headed toward the exit.

Michelle smiled and cocked her head. "Do you really think I'd like it out here?"

"Baby, I found the perfect spot in Laguna. It's made for you, and they'll love your art." He cupped her face, the heat of his fingers danced over her cheek. "Does that mean you'll stay?"

She gulped and nodded. "Yeah, I'll give it a try."

Hunter pulled her into his arms hugging her tight. "That's all I can ask. I can't believe I almost lost you." His breath was heavy on her hair as he loosened his embrace. He hooked his thumb under her chin. "I love you. With every fiber of my being. I'm nothing without you." He brushed his lips over hers and she melted into his arms.

Moaning into his mouth, her fingers brushed through his hair. His taste instantly transported her to the night they shared. Liquid heat pooled between her thighs, and she squeezed her legs together to find relief to her throbbing sex. "Let's get out of here. Now."

Hunter stood and held out his hands, which she met with her own. Pulling her up, he wrapped his arms around her again. "I'll never leave you again. I promise."

"I'll never let you," she said as she snuggled into the crook of his arm.

Hunter hung his arm around her shoulder and wheeled her suitcase with the other as they left the terminal.

Chapter Twenty-One

Michelle's phone vibrated in her pocket. Pulling it out, she glanced at Miranda's text.

What flight are you on? I'll pick you up at the airport.

She smiled and tapped back: *False alarm. I'm staying. I'll call you in the morning. Love you.*

"Everything okay?" Hunter asked, squeezing her shoulder.

"Yeah, everything's fine. More than fine." They stopped in front of the parking garage elevator and Hunter pushed the up button. Michelle looked from her phone to Hunter. "If you didn't see me outside your apartment, how did you know I was even here?"

Hunter chuckled. "Alex called me and ripped me a new asshole. He tried to give me a heads-up earlier by telling me a surprise was waiting for me when I got home from work. I figured he signed me up for the Jelly of the Month club."

Michelle laughed. "How did Alex know? I only called Miranda."

Hunter shrugged. "She must've called Alex and gave him an earful."

"Miranda and Alex, huh? It would be interesting if they got back together." Michelle looked up at Hunter and winked.

"Miranda is perfect for Alex. He needs someone who won't take his crap."

Stepping off the elevator, Michelle searched the virtually abandoned parking deck. "What made you park up here?"

Hunter took her hand in his, intertwining his fingers between her own as they walked in the direction of a lone car partially blocked by a cement pillar. "I knew I'd find a spot here and it was faster to park quick and run to the terminal." He shot her a sly smile. "But now I'm thinking of another benefit for parking up here."

"And what might that be?" Michelle asked, meeting his grin with her own.

Hunter turned and encircled her waist between his hands. Stepping forward he slowly backed her against the cement pillar. His fingers slid under the seam of her shirt and rubbed warm circles along the skin of her hip. "We both know how great make-up sex is. I hear make-up sex with the risk of getting caught is even better."

"Here?" she asked, pointing to the pillar she leaned against.

"There." His finger pointed in the direction of the Nova. Hunter's mouth inched closer as he spoke. His fingers trailed up her side to the nape of her neck. Gathering her hair into his fist, he pulled, causing her chin to lift and exposing her neck. He kissed the sensitive skin along her jawbone, moving closer to her ear. "I need you here and now."

Michelle bucked her hips, grinding her sex against his thigh. "I'm not arguing."

Hunter's lips found hers as his tongue searched her mouth for answers. She responded with a caress from her tongue. His touch claimed her body. "You're mine. Always. Mine."

Michelle moaned in his mouth in response. Swallowing hard, she broke their kiss and gazed into his eyes. Her fingers traced his face and rubbed against the scruff at his jawbone. "I never thought I'd touch you again." Her fingertips danced over his neck to his T-shirt-covered chest. He was so warm, hard, and alive. She palmed his chest and felt the beat of his heart at her fingertips. A sudden need to feel his skin against hers overcame her, and she hooked her fingers under the seam of his shirt and pulled it over his head. Her hands slid down his back as she pulled him close.

"Car. Now." He took her hands into his, guiding her to the car while kissing her neck. Gently backing her against the door, Hunter's low growl warmed her core as he unbuttoned her jeans and slipped his hand into the waistband. He drew down the zipper as his weight shifted and the car door opened. He pulled her up and wrapped her long hair around his fist. "Damn it, Michelle. I missed your smell. I missed your taste." He swiveled her around and kissed her hard, guiding her to the opened door.

He pulled her shirt over her head before helping her into the car. They were partially hidden between the corner wall and a concrete pillar. Hunter looked around quickly before crouching in front of her, rubbing the legs of her jeans. "Lift up for me." She lifted her hips as he yanked her jeans over her ass and pulled them to her feet. He threw the garment into the front seat and surveyed her body with a hooded gaze. "I didn't think I'd get to do this again."

She crooked her finger, gesturing him to join her in the backseat. Unbuttoning his own jeans with one hand, he leaned over her until they were both lying hot and ready on the upholstered back seat. She pulled her top over her head and unsnapped her bra. He kissed a line from her neck to her chest, lifting each soft globe from the cups of her bra before taking her hardened nipple into his mouth.

She moaned and raked her hands through his hair. "Hunter," she whispered as his thumb found her other nipple. She bucked her hips to meet his jean-covered rigid sex.

He smiled wickedly and left an erotic trail of licks, nips, and kisses down her stomach. "I need to taste you." He reached her lace-covered mound as his body slid partially outside the car. The thrill of getting caught combined with his breath heavy on her sex flooded her core and dampened the crotch of her panties. He lightly kissed and rubbed his fingers over the sensitive skin of her inner thigh. She lifted her hips, but he pinned them to the seat. "Don't move but lift up on your elbows. I want you to watch me bring you to the edge. I need to see your face."

She leaned on her elbows and their gaze met as footsteps filled the silence. He lifted his index finger to his lips. She smiled at him. Never in her life did she ever imagine she'd be in the parking garage at LAX doing nasty things with a man like him.

The footsteps stopped and a car door opened and closed before an engine turned over.

"I think the coast is clear. Now where was I?" He raised his eyebrows. "Ah, now I remember."

Michelle giggled.

He pushed the strip of lace aside, her sex pink and wet. He parted her legs until her knees were against the backseat and the front. His tongue trailed a wet line up the outer lips of her sex, and she threw her head back as heat rushed to her core.

"I said I want you to watch me, Michelle."

She forced her head forward, her hair covering one eye. "Hunter, please."

"Please what, baby. I want to hear what you want."

"Take me with your tongue. Consume me. Anything you want. Make me yours."

His fingers trailed a line down her sex as she spoke while his tongue found her sensitive bundle of nerves. His fingers and mouth worked in tandem, pumping into her as she came closer and closer to the edge. It was difficult for her to keep her eyes open. "Stay with me, Michelle."

She panted and reached out to touch his face as he continued to pleasure her. "Hunter. I'm going to—"

He replaced his finger with his tongue, tracing a circle around her pearl, applying more pressure each turn. "Let yourself go off the edge."

She ran her fingers through his hair. "Hunter." Her inner walls contracted around his fingers as he pumped into her, milking her release until she lay back, spent and sated. He moved over her body, kissing her skin with warmth and love as he found her mouth. She kissed him as her hands moved to his waist and palmed at his jeans.

He pulled them down and took a foil pocket from his jeans and sheathed himself. "Turn around, baby."

She flipped around so that her knees pushed against the upholstery. He moved behind her, positioning his length along her sex. Cupping her breast, he guided his erection into her channel. They moaned together as he thrust into her core, filling her. Her cheek melded to the seat of the car as hot breath bathed her neck.

"Fuck, Michelle. You're mine. Say it, baby."

"Always."

He bit the skin of her shoulder softly. She called out from the sensation of his mouth and his length moving inside her. His hand slid from her breast down her stomach to her hot sex, finding the spot he so expertly maneuvered only moments ago. He touched her as he continued to pump from behind. "God, you feel so good."

A bell dinged from beyond as the sound of an elevator climbing the floors chugged.

"Hunter. Someone's coming."

"That would be me, sweetheart."

Michelle giggled. "No, really. Someone's in the garage. You have to stop for a moment."

"I can't stop now." His movements came slower and he moaned in her ear.

"Shit," she said. "Oh God." Her core tightened around his length as a strong release overtook her body.

Hunter groaned deep in her ear. "Oh, love, I think you like taking risks." He pumped harder as he joined her in climax." He rocked her slowly until her inner walls relaxed. Her hair stuck to her face and a light sheen of sweat covered her exposed skin.

"I think we should get out of here before we get arrested." Michelle reached behind her finding his cheek. "I have plans for you, McAvery, and they won't materialize if we're both in separate jail cells."

Hunter laughed and crawled out of the backseat, removing the condom and zipping up his pants. "Shit. Michelle. Get dressed, fast."

Heavy footsteps approached the car as Michelle slid on her pants and shirt.

"Where's my shirt?" he whispered.

"I think we left it outside," she said, trying hard not to laugh.

"Sir," a voice echoed through the parking deck.

"Yeah, hi there, officer." Hunter walked around the car, blocking the window to the backseat.

"Where's your shirt, sir?"

"My shirt? It seems my shirt is right here, officer."

Michelle peeked out the window to see Hunter bend down and pick up his T-shirt from the ground and pull it on over his head.

"Who's in the car?"

"It's my girlfriend, officer. We got a little carried away. We're just leaving."

The officer craned his neck around Hunter to look inside the car. "Miss, I'm going to have to ask you to get out of the car. After you're decent, of course."

She fastened her jeans and ran her fingers through her hair, not that it'd help much. She pulled open the door and climbed out of the backseat. Heat rose in her cheeks.

The officer cleared his throat. "I just need to know this man is not keeping you here under duress."

"No, sir. I'm here by my free will. It's been a while since we've seen each other." She glanced at Hunter and a smile formed on her face.

"Well, you're not the first couple to try this, and you certainly won't be the last. Do us all a favor and go home before a video of your escapades ends up trending on the Internet."

"Yes, sir. I'll be happy to get her home."

"I'm sure you will." The officer looked at Hunter and Michelle before smiling and turning toward the stairwell. He pulled his radio from his belt. "All clear."

Hunter and Michelle looked at each other and burst out in laughter. Hunter grabbed her and wrapped his arms around her shoulders. "That'll be one to tell our kids," he said playfully.

"Kids? You're getting ahead of yourself, aren't you?"

"Get used to it. I'll never let you out of my sight again. How about we take a ride through Laguna? There's a coffee shop out there that makes the best peanut butter chocolate chip cookies."

The End

www.sandrabunino.com

Evernight Publishing

www.evernightpublishing.com